*A scientist by background, **Moira Curry** over 25 years, with responsibility for Scie. in the schools where she taught.*

Moira has now left paid teaching to devote more time to children's work, and to develop her role with a small UK charity that works alongside an economically deprived village community in Uganda. Part of her church worship team, she is also a trained listener and tutor for Acorn Christian Healing Trust. Married to Richard, with three grown-up children, Moira enjoys singing, creative textile work, producing handmade books, walking and swimming.

***Gill Morgan** grew up in Chester and trained as a primary school teacher, specialising in music. Married to Gareth, she taught for three years before leaving to concentrate on bringing up their four children, now grown up. After several years running music workshops for preschool children, Gill returned to teaching, spending ten years teaching RE, Music and Arts in a village school.*

Since 2000 Gill and Gareth have been involved with a development programme for a village in Eastern Uganda, the growth of which contributed to her giving up teaching in 2003. Gill and Moira import and sell crafts from Uganda to support the projects, as well as giving promotional presentations. Gill and Gareth are local leaders for The Marriage Course. *Gill's interests include cooking for family and friends, gardening, walking, photography and creative textile work. Her chocolate brownie is legendary.*

Moira and Gill have been involved in a range of children's activities in their church and community, including lunch, after-school and holiday clubs, and have been part of the children's team at Spring Harvest. They are also Scripture Union affiliates and have trialled new material for the organisation. The development of this work led them into heading up the Christmas Journey *and* Easter Journey *teams at Main St Community Church in Frodsham, Cheshire.*

Text copyright © Moira Curry and Gill Morgan 2009
Illustrations copyright © tbc 2009
The authors assert the moral right
to be identified as the authors of this work

Published by
The Bible Reading Fellowship
15 The Chambers, Vineyard
Abingdon OX14 3FE
United Kingdom
Tel: +44 (0)1865 319700
Email: enquiries@brf.org.uk
Website: www.brf.org.uk

ISBN 978 1 84101 621 4
First published 2009
10 9 8 7 6 5 4 3 2 1 0
All rights reserved

Acknowledgments
Unless otherwise stated, scripture quotations are taken from the Contemporary English Version
of the Bible published by HarperCollins Publishers, copyright © 1991, 1992, 1995 American
Bible Society.

Scripture quotations taken from the Holy Bible, New International Version, copyright © 1973,
1978, 1984, 1995 by International Bible Society. Used by permission of Hodder & Stoughton,
a division of Hodder Headline Ltd. All rights reserved. 'NIV' is a registered trademark of
International Bible Society. UK trademark number 148790.

A catalogue record for this book is available from the British Library

Printed in Singapore by Craft Print International Ltd

The Christmas Journey

An imaginative presentation
for churches to use with primary schools

Moira Curry and Gill Morgan

★ To our long-suffering husbands, for your much-appreciated support, encouragement and practical help in all we do—even though we know you would sometimes rather be on the golf course!
★

Acknowledgments

Thanks go to Helen Franklin, whose encouragement and belief in us has sent us on many exciting 'journeys' over the years, including this one.

Thank you, too, to Martin Ansdell-Smith for so generously sharing his expertise in setting up and maintaining the *Christmas Journey* website.

To all those who have given support, skills and advice in the putting together of the book, we are truly grateful.

Thank you to Martyn Payne for his invaluable help and inspiration.

Finally, and most importantly, heartfelt thanks go to the entire *Christmas Journey* team, each one of you making your own very special contribution, and without whom none of this could have happened.

Comments on The Christmas Journey experience

We would particularly like to commend The Christmas Journey *experience. It was lovely that in the midst of all the hustle and bustle and glitz of the festival, there was time for a quieter reflection at this time of Christmas.*
HEAD TEACHER

The Christmas presentation at Main Street was an incredible experience for our infant children and one that they will not forget. I have been taking my Year Two children to The Christmas Journey *at Main Street Chapel for three years. I'm always impressed by the excellent team who organize and run the journey and the way, through storytellers, puppets and actors, they bring alive this amazing story.*
YEAR TWO TEACHER

The children feel part of the journey by singing songs, following the star to distant lands, visiting Mary and hearing her good news, dressing up as shepherds and travelling to the stable to meet some friends. The children are enthralled as they use their senses and become part of this extraordinary journey.
YEAR TWO TEACHER

It was magical. I liked the bit where we saw the puppets in the stable and they made us giggle!
KATIE, AGED 7, YEAR TWO PUPIL

I loved it! We saw the sky moving and followed the star to see Mary and I got a shock when Angel Gabriel came round the corner!
OLIVIA, AGED 6, YEAR TWO PUPIL

I liked dressing up as a wise man and smelling the frankincense.
HARVEY, AGED 6, YEAR TWO PUPIL

As a teacher of autistic children I wondered what they would think of their visit to The Christmas Journey. *I shouldn't have worried—they loved it! The journey was a multisensory experience which they really enjoyed. During the journey they listened to stories linked to objects of reference. They tasted freshly made bread, wore shepherds' headdresses and smelt the exotic spices in the wise men's palace. Their favourite part, however, was to meet and listen to the animals in the stable. It was a great way to find out and learn about the nativity story.*
SPECIAL NEEDS TEACHER

It totally enhances the work we do in school and gives scope for follow-up work. I have, for instance, retold The Christmas Journey *in storyboard format.*
DEPUTY HEAD TEACHER

It is wonderful to have this spiritual input and remind the children about the actual reason for Christmas, since there are so many commercial pressures. Talk of 'what they are getting' seems to dominate their thoughts.
DEPUTY HEAD TEACHER

I enjoy being part of the Christmas Journey *team and even take time off work to join in doing whatever part is needed. I bake bread, help with the children and have sometimes filled in as a puppeteer. It's wonderful to see the children's faces as they travel round.*
MEMBER OF *THE CHRISTMAS JOURNEY* TEAM

Taking part in The Christmas Journey *is, for me, a real joy and privilege. As puppeteers we can often hear the children's reactions to the story and these can be amusing. We sometimes have a hard job suppressing our laughter.*
MEMBER OF *THE CHRISTMAS JOURNEY* TEAM

Listening to the children as they go round and being part of the team really strengthens my faith.

MEMBER OF *THE CHRISTMAS JOURNEY* TEAM

I really like the way that The Christmas Journey *also gives children an idea of God's wider plans, as it begins with creation and finishes with the new beginning of Easter. And so, there are questions to ponder even for those children who are already familiar with the events of the first Christmas.*

MEMBER OF *THE CHRISTMAS JOURNEY* TEAM

The Christmas Journey *is an extremely important part of the outreach of Main Street Community Church. As someone who came to the church after the event began, I see how it has impacted our community with the incarnation story, impressing even school teachers who were ambivalent to the Christian faith. For the church, it provides a role for everyone, not just those with dramatic talent. Whether on the forefront or on the sidelines, every volunteer enjoys witnessing the excitement and surprise of the children as they experience the event. This is not a 'reaping' event but one in which we sow seeds in lives of children and adults alike. I recommend it to any church wishing to positively impact their community.*

CHURCH LEADER

Contents

Part One

Part Two

Part Three

Foreword

What do you remember of childhood Christmases? Well, obviously that it was much colder and crisper than now—distance always lends enchantment—and probably that it snowed, too! But what magical experiences spring to mind? A visit to meet Father Christmas in his grotto… a trip to the pantomime… a part in the school nativity play?

The Christmas Journey offers just the same tingling experience, but one that increases children's knowledge of the story of Jesus' birth and their understanding of why there was a need for God's Son to become one of us. You will not find any of the 'add-ons' of Christmas here (fun though a jolly man in a red suit may be). This experience takes children right to the heart of the nativity story. Nor will they will meet a girl dressed as a handsome prince, or a man dressed as the mother, but God clothed in human form. And rather than cries of 'He's behind you!' the truth they will discover is 'He's with you!' as they see, hear, touch, taste and smell their way round this most tremendous tale of all.

As you read the following pages, you might feel 'Well, it's all right for them: they're so capable, they've even written a book about it!' Moira and Gill have immense skills and talents, but the key factor is that they love God, understand children and want to bring the two together. That they have done this through *The Christmas Journey* is not down to their skills alone but also to God's work. May you know the presence and power of Immanuel, 'God with us', as you walk *The Christmas Journey* with the children and families of your area and offer them the opportunity to experience the wonder of the birth of Jesus.

Helen Franklin
Regional Manager for Scripture Union, and children's worker

Introduction

The Christmas story is not new. It is at least 2000 years old and, even at the beginning, was probably told in many different forms. The excited shepherds, having been woken from sleep and interrupted by angels on a very ordinary working night, may have run back to their bewildered families with their own versions of the story. Bethlehem would have been buzzing.

As Jesus grew up, Mary and Joseph had an amazing story to tell him about the extraordinary circumstances surrounding his birth. The wise men most certainly would have written their story in their learned astrological documents. The disciples and early church members would no doubt have heard the story as it was passed down the generations, and the Holy Spirit inspired two of the Gospel writers to pass it on for us to read today.

This amazing story—God becoming a human being, a child like us, entering our world as a vulnerable baby—has led to many and various imaginative portrayals as we try to take in the enormity of the event. Artists, playwrights, songwriters and actors have all played their part in bringing us the story that we know today. Enter many of our nation's primary schools at Christmas and you will find a sea of white frilly angels, masked donkeys, tea-towelled shepherds and splendidly robed wise men, putting on that timeless story, watched by proud parents and carers. Many a Christmas carol has painted a picture of the extraordinary story—some more extraordinary than others. It is hard to believe that the young Jesus never cried and was really 'mild and obedient' all the time. Even more difficult to picture is Mary giving birth in a stable surrounded by Italian Renaissance palaces. The events of Christmas were considered so important, however, that they were written into the culture of many generations and even now, centuries later, we still celebrate the birth of this baby.

The Christmas journey portrayed in this book is not original;

it is possibly not much different from many more professional productions, for there is no 'right' way to tell the story. The presentation set out here is offered to local schools and the community as an experience, so that those taking part in the story may enter into the wonder and mystery of the elements of the event. *The Christmas Journey* does not end with Jesus in the manger but is portrayed as God's rescue plan for the world. We hope that, having entered into the experience, both children and adults will understand that Christmas is part of a much bigger story, which is still being played out today.

This book is designed as a tool kit to enable churches to run their own presentation and is supported by *The Christmas Journey* website, www.christmasjourney.org.uk, where additional information can be accessed. On the website there are photographs, plans and downloads available.

The book is divided into three sections. The first part describes the background and practical planning needed before the experience. There are hints about team training, enthusing the church family, publicity and links with schools. The second part gives a practical outline of the components of the event. There are lists of props, scenery and characters, together with scripts and suggestions for lighting. The third section develops ideas for follow-up activities once schools have visited the presentation, to help to keep the experience alive. There are ideas for all-age worship, assemblies and class lessons as well as further resources to complement the visit.

The outline

When visiting *The Christmas Journey*, children and adults are led around key elements of the traditional story in a thought-provoking way, by leaders trained to help the participants respond at their own level of understanding. *The Christmas Journey* is multisensory, lasts about three-quarters of an hour and can be adapted to different buildings and spaces. Essentially, there are six storytelling rooms or scenes, which relate to different parts of the Christmas story. Each room develops part of the story. Groups are led on a journey beginning with an interpretation of the story of creation using visual materials. The story then moves to Mary's kitchen, on to the shepherds' hillside and then to the stable in Bethlehem. A visit to the wise men's palace completes the traditional Christmas story and children are then invited to a modern-day living room to reflect on the experience. Here the story focuses on Jesus' ministry and the final week of his life, leading to the concept that Christmas is only the start of God's rescue plan for the world and that the story goes on.

The presentation is designed primarily for Year Two children, so that schools may be invited annually. Year Two was chosen as the focus on the basis that, by this age, most children are familiar with the basics of the Christmas story and are beginning to develop thinking skills and questioning the world they inhabit. The expectation is that the same children will experience *The Easter Journey* when they reach Year Five. Therefore, *The Christmas Journey* is related to *The Easter Journey*, which is a separate but similar event designed for older children.

The Christmas Journey in its original setting, in the Cheshire town of Frodsham, is run as part of a town Christmas festival, so it is open to the general public at the weekend. The leaders are therefore encouraged to adapt their explanation to encompass a wider age group. Children experiencing *The Christmas Journey* during school time frequently return with their families at the weekend, creating an encouraging response. Linking the weekend presentation with invitations to an all-age worship service based on *The Christmas Journey* means that we have an excellent tool for reaching out into the community.

Much of the content of the book is based on the experience of running *The Christmas Journey* in a small church in Frodsham. Anyone reading the book and wanting to run the event themselves will no doubt approach the project from different situations and with different opportunities. However, it may be useful and encouraging to hear our story of how God blessed this germ of an idea and led us on our own faith journey, both as individuals and as a team, from very small beginnings.

The journey begins

Although we as a church are not part of a recognized denomination, we have links in the area with many different churches. The local Anglican diocese has a regular bulletin of events that may interest others in the area and, on one occasion, we noticed a presentation of the Easter story was due to take place in Crewe. Something about this struck a chord, so we decided to go along and have a look.

In phoning to arrange our visit, we discovered that the organizer was someone we'd met the previous year on the children's work team at Spring Harvest, thus giving us an ideal opportunity to stay afterwards and talk over the presentation with her. The event revealed a happy atmosphere of primary school children alongside keen and willing volunteers portraying the story of that first Easter in a variety of different ways, including drama, language and song. Afterwards we learnt more about the relationship that the church had been building up with local schools, and how they put on not only an Easter journey but also a Christmas event along similar lines.

As we drove back to Frodsham, there was plenty of time to talk over what we had seen. We were part of a team that had been praying for local schools for over 15 years, and we had certainly seen some answers to prayer. Could this be another link in that chain? We both felt that we needed to explore prayerfully what God might be saying—both feeling a mixture of excitement and dread at what was being asked of us. Various members of the Frodsham churches had worked together at events such as holiday clubs, schools' clubs and so on at different times, and we felt that this could be another such venture.

Exploring the idea

We decided that we would start by exploring a way to present the Christmas journey; we felt that Christmas was more readily recognized by schools as a time when they might want to come along to a special event. The previous year, our town had held a Christmas festival—a civic-run event that had involved the whole town in a variety of activities, none of which, though fun to be part of, had any direct link with the events of the first Christmas. We realized that a presentation of the Christmas journey could be a way for local churches to offer something to the festival.

Together we talked over various ways of staging the event. The presentation in Crewe had taken place in a traditional Baptist building, which was large and had lots of available space for a variety of uses. Our church building in Frodsham was much smaller and more modern. However, despite having less room, we felt that the space might be more adaptable. We realized that to use the corners of the main worship area would allow the remaining space in the middle of the room to be used as an additional area. Our initial thought was to arrange for some sort of wooden structures to be built, which would be collapsible and easily put away for future use. The inevitable bulkiness of such a structure, however, caused us to think that this idea might be impractical. Thus began a series of events, which seemed to confirm to us that God was leading us further.

The first steps

A few weeks later, we came upon a shop that had a special offer on gazebos (the sort of structure most often used to accommodate guests at a wet barbecue). The gazebos were square, green, well-made metal structures and were a real bargain. It was time to consider how serious we both were about the *Christmas Journey* idea. Should we invest in four gazebos, as they would be a good, flexible and easily stored way of using the four corners of our area? We decided that they were worth snapping up: even if nothing came of the plans to develop the idea of a presentation of the Christmas story, there would be plenty of people likely to be hosting barbecues that summer who would be willing to take one off our hands.

About this time (mid-June), the town's Christmas festival planning meetings got under way. We asked if we could be included and were welcomed with open arms: our position as representatives of the churches in the town was recognized as very helpful in the planning of a Christmas festival. This contact proved invaluable, since, at one of the subsequent meetings, the question of funding was being discussed. We threw in the comment that if there were spare funds available, perhaps they could help us with transport costs, so that schools could be offered transport free of charge to and from their visit to *The Christmas Journey*. To our amazement, it was unanimously decided that the town council would pay for the bus, which meant that the church could operate one bus to tour several schools, collecting and delivering the children to fit in with the schedule for their visit to the presentation. Excellent news!

We knew that it was time to bring the leaders of our church up to date with the developments in our plans for *The Christmas Journey*. Although we had done many things involving schools in the past, this was to be our most ambitious project to date. As we expected, our church leaders were very supportive, offering encouragement, prayer, and—just as importantly—church funds to cover costs where necessary.

Gathering the team

Realizing that we could not stage the event alone, it was time to see who would be interested in helping to form a full team to run the project. Like many churches, we have people who are capable of great things but have a natural reserve—a modesty that can hamper progress. Our church has a strong history of working with other churches in the town, so the plans and ideas were taken along to the *Churches Together* meeting, where they were received with overwhelming support, with many people interested in joining the team. With some encouragement along the way to those with 'natural reserve', we had a good attendance at the first *Christmas Journey* team meeting.

This first meeting was held in October to discuss the initial idea and where to go from there. The response was wholly encouraging and afterwards we felt that God was giving us the 'go-ahead'. The project had turned from an idea with a bit of potential into a feasible proposition and we knew it was time to step out in faith and go ahead and plan the event.

This first meeting was the catalyst, the blue touchpaper which was about to be lit. We had presented the idea to our potential team with full awareness that it was only the germ of an idea; it was to be true teamwork that changed our idea into a working proposition. Among other things we discussed at that initial meeting was the fact that the experience would need to be multisensory. It was suggested that it would be a good idea to use puppets to tell part of the story, and one of our church members mentioned that her brother ran a toy shop and had some animal puppets that might just fit the bill. Further enquiries proved this to be the case: there are more details on the website, www.christmasjourney.org.uk.

God confirms the plans

During the development of the initial plans, a Bible verse was repeatedly coming to the fore. In Matthew 13 Jesus tells the parable of the farmer, in which some of his seed falls along the road and is eaten by birds. Other seed falls on thin, rocky ground and is dried up because the soil isn't very deep. More seeds fall where thorn bushes grow up and choke the plants. But a few seeds fall on good ground where the plants produce 100 or 60 or 30 times as much as was scattered. As we reflected on this parable and read on, we felt that God was saying, 'This next bit applies to you and what I am asking you to do with *The Christmas Journey*'.

Matthew 13:35 says, 'I will use stories to speak my message and to explain things that have been hidden since the creation of the world.' This verse seemed to be saying that here was an ideal opportunity to spread God's word (the seed) through the retelling of the great story of his plan for humankind. We subsequently used this verse on *The Christmas Journey* prayer cards (see page 38 for further information).

A smaller team planned the storyboard for the event. Each person there made a valuable contribution and the main components of *The Christmas Journey* were soon in place: Mary's kitchen, where the angel would come and give her the amazing news of what would happen to her; the hillside where the shepherds would be told that a baby had been born; the stable where we would hear all about the arrival of that baby; and the wise men's palace, where we would find out all about the journey that these learned people were about to take. However, there were two missing components. The four scenarios just described would be familiar, we hoped, to many of those coming on the journey, but the first Christmas was part of a bigger picture, a wider plan, and it was essential to include both the beginning (creation) and the 'ongoing end' (God's plan of salvation for his world). How could these two elements be put across? We knew that this would have to be done in a special way, so that the event would be more than yet another retelling of the story of the first Christmas.

On the weekend immediately following the planning meeting, there was a reunion with old friends from youth fellowship days. One of these friends had experience of working with schools and churches within the context of the Christian faith. While we were talking together over that weekend, he agreed to help in the planning of the two missing elements: creation and God's plan of salvation.

Experienced in presenting creative storytelling, this friend was able to help to write those two sections of *The Christmas Journey*.

Moving on

With the main components of *The Christmas Journey* in place, other issues needed to be addressed. Our church at Frodsham is small—fewer than 50 people attend most Sunday mornings—yet talent lay hidden beneath the surface. The scenery was painted by one of the members. A script was written for the stable (reproduced in this book and on the website); a friend from another church just 'happened' to know someone with an Indian mother-in-law who was happy to lend a box full of saris to drape in the wise men's palace.

All these events further confirmed that we were progressing in the right direction. One last thing was needed: we hoped to find a small take-home gift for the children, such as a book that told the Christmas story simply, yet packed enough punch to give the whole picture. Despite visiting local Christian bookshops, asking around among other contacts and trawling websites, nothing seemed suitable. In a completely different context (a meeting with a friend who ran a campaign in Manchester called 'Real Christmas'), a little book came to light that hit the nail right on the head. Called *Meet the Cast*, it told the story of the first Christmas through the characters involved. These characters were drawn in a simple cartoon style, and we found that the visuals from the booklet could be downloaded from the website of the book suppliers, Lifewords (formerly Scripture Gift Mission: see Resources section for contact details). This was the final piece of the jigsaw. We could use these symbolic characters to 'brand' *The Christmas Journey* and give it a logo (something that we considered to be an important component).

From the downloads we developed a logo to appear on our letters to schools, on our prayer cards, and on the T-shirts for the team to wear. Since there are plain windows at the front of our church, which face on to the main street of the town, a member of the congregation painted a selection of the characters and the logo on to the windows. This served as publicity and an invitation to the public to come and join *The Christmas Journey*.

There was still just one more vital element. Without school children to attend, all the work would be in vain. We were fortunate enough to have an established relationship with the local primary schools, partly because our own children attended two of them and partly because we had both recently finished working in another two. As soon as schools heard about *The Christmas Journey*, they quickly signed up to come.

If you have not yet established a relationship with your local schools, see page 39 for some suggestions on how to do so. Schools nowadays are expected to be part of a cluster, working with other schools in many areas, and head teachers will readily recommend events to other heads.

There were many other affirmations in the inevitable moments of panic as we took on this task, but the support of the churches, the participation of the team members, the faces of the children and the response of the adult visitors have made *The Christmas Journey* a very special event in the life of our church and community. Our tentative small steps have been richly blessed.

Part One

★

Framework of the presentation

The Christmas Journey is designed so that the whole experience lasts for an hour, suitable for groups of up to 30 children.

When they first arrive, visitors are asked to sit down in a suitable area and are welcomed to *The Christmas Journey*. Once seated, the group is welcomed and pupils are taught the theme song, 'Where are you going, shepherds?' Words and music are available on page 97 and on the website. The children are told to look out for the characters mentioned in the song as they travel round the journey. It may be useful to have a second song to hand, such as 'Christmas Hokey Cokey' (*Christmas Wrapped Up*, SU 2003), in case delaying tactics are needed. Have the words available on a flipchart, OHP or PowerPoint projector. The songs could have guitar or keyboard accompaniment if available.

After this, the leader explains that the children will be split in two groups, one to begin *The Christmas Journey* and the second to remain where they are to take part in a craft activity. It is advisable to ask teachers to divide the group, as they often have firm ideas about which children should be together and which adults should accompany the children.

The first group is then introduced to a guide, who explains to the children that they are going on a wonderful journey. He or she leads the group to the entrance of the presentation area, building up an air of mystery and excitement before they enter the first scene. Guides could hold something for the children to follow, such as a torch or battery-operated star. Soft music playing and appropriate lighting can create an air of anticipation and expectation.

At a signal that all is ready, the first group is taken into the presentation area and *The Christmas Journey* begins.

Craft activity

Once the first group have left for the journey, the second group are ready to start their craft activity. Children will enjoy having something they have made to take home as a reminder of *The Christmas Journey*. A leader will explain the process to the whole group, who move to tables where team members are waiting to assist the children. Help will be needed beforehand to design the craft, buy and organize materials and prepare tables.

Tables are laid out with materials for the children to use, and helpers can use the time to chat with the children. The craft activity itself needs to take no longer than eight or ten minutes, so it needs to be fairly prescribed and simple. However, it is important that the finished item is pleasing and as individual as possible, offering some choice in the creative process. The craft item can change year-to-year depending on the creativity of the team and availability of materials. A simple Christmas card works well. Provide pre-cut shapes to glue on to the card and some opportunity for colouring or using stickers or glitter pens, which can all produce a pleasing effect. If you do develop a logo, it may be possible to incorporate it into the card.

It is important that each child's work is named, especially if you have more than one school at a session, to ensure that each school receives the correct items on departure. Producing sticky labels on the computer with the school name and *The Christmas Journey* logo takes a little time, but gives a professional appearance.

An important part of this session is also to provide a comfortable waiting area for the school staff who accompany each group, so that they are able to have coffee and tea and look at resources suitable for RE and Citizenship. Teachers are normally responsible for children for the whole of an educational visit, so a short break, in a place where they can still see the children but are being looked after themselves, can be very welcome. This is a useful time for the team leaders or church minister to chat to the visiting staff, explaining *The Christmas Journey* and perhaps offering help with assemblies linked to this or other Christian events if they feel able to.

It is worth thinking about adding other experiences to *The Christmas Journey*, so that if children finish their craft activity quickly (and some will!) there is something else for them to do. In Frodsham, a display of nativity sets from around the world has provided an added attraction for the helpers to show the children. These are readily available from fair trade organizations such as Tearcraft, Traidcraft, Oxfam and so on, and a plea for the congregation to lend sets can be very productive. Some sets can be fragile and it is important that children are asked to respect this fact. It is worth providing a couple of more robust sets on a separate table for the children to handle and play with. A basket of appropriate children's Christmas storybooks in a cosy corner with rugs and cushions is also useful. The local library can provide books if given enough notice.

Once the second group, with their teachers, have departed on *The Christmas Journey*, the helpers can prepare the tables again with materials for the return of the first group.

For the final scene, the children are led out of the last gazebo into a lounge area outside the main hall. This creates a feeling of travelling forward in time from a darkened area into the light of the present day.

Sample timetable for one school visit

Ideally, each scene should take about six minutes, but some scenes may take longer than others—particularly those that are interactive. The guides need to make sure that they keep to time because the second group needs to begin the journey when the first group enters the shepherds' scene.

Approximate time	Group 1	Group 2
9.30am	Welcome and song	Welcome and song
9.40am	In the beginning	Crafts/exhibit
9.46am	Mary's kitchen	Crafts/exhibit

9.52am	A hillside near Bethlehem	In the beginning
9.58am	Stable	Mary's kitchen
10.04am	Palace	A hillside near Bethlehem
10.10am	The new beginning	Stable
10.16am	Crafts/exhibit	Palace
10.22am	Crafts/exhibit	The new beginning

Although this timetable looks very precise, bear in mind that it is just a guide and you need to allow for a little flexibility. Much will depend on the size and responsiveness of the group. However, guides do need to be aware of the time, particularly when using the same storyteller for both groups, so that he or she has time to get in place for the last scene.

Each scene is described in detail on pages 54–95.

Suggested daily timetable for several school visits

As *The Christmas Journey* experience lasts for just one hour, there will be time for up to four school groups to visit per day. The morning sessions will last from 9.30am until 10.30am and 10.45am until 11.45am, which allows for a short changeover slot. Afternoon sessions will run from 12.45pm until 1.45pm, then 1.45pm until 2.45pm, allowing pupils to return to school for home time. At Frodsham, the schools attending the 12.45pm slot would often arrange for the pupils attending to have an early lunch that day. It is also worth considering the proximity of the final school of the day, perhaps giving a warning just in case the event overruns by a few minutes.

9.00 am	Team meet for prayer and preparation
9.30–10.30 am	School 1
10.45–11.45 am	School 2
12.45–1.45pm	School 3
1.45–2.45pm	School 4

If several schools are visiting in one day, there are several important points to consider, to make sure the day runs smoothly.

- Try to use a one-way system of entrances and exits if your building allows for this, so that if one school arrives as another is leaving, there is no confusion.
- A holding area is useful, so that if a school arrives early, there will be time to sing a familiar song or even watch part of a suitable video without disturbing the previous school.
- The children need a place to remove and store coats. If a one-way system is used for arrival and departure, it is helpful if coats are moved to the exit at an appropriate time during the event.

✱

Preparing for the event: the church community

Once you have decided to put on *The Christmas Journey* yourself, there are several considerations to take into account. As Christians, we are inviting schools to take part in an event that shows the church community working together to produce an experience that is both exciting and of a high standard. Schools have come to expect sophisticated, high-tech events and our task is to present the Christmas story in an attractive, professional way without detracting from the biblical narrative. This can be a good opportunity to show your local community that the church is relevant and up to date.

Creating a team

The event will need a team of enthusiastic people who are able to work together to provide an exciting and thought-provoking experience for the visitors. If your church is small, you could invite other churches to work together to expand the team. *Churches Together* or a similar local group would be a good platform from which to share the vision and recruit helpers. It may be useful to ask for time in Sunday services at other churches to explain the idea and encourage helpers. Notice sheets, church magazines and personal invitations can be effective. It is important that the church community should provide an experience for schools that is both enjoyable and professional. Working together with other Christians as part of the team can be a real blessing to those involved as well as a valuable witness to visitors.

So, then, what kind of a team is needed to put on *The Christmas Journey*? The lists below suggest the need for a huge team of people both before and during the event. If people are in short supply, however, many of these roles can be doubled up: some of them are required only for short periods of time. Assigning helpers to a specific job or jobs helps the team to have clarity of purpose and a feeling of value and responsibility. Once a list of specific tasks is drawn up, you will be amazed at the skills that people feel they can offer. The church family can develop ownership of the event and use many gifts and skills in preparation.

Helpers needed in preparation for the event

- Leader/coordinator(s): This could be one person or a small team, but it is essential that those involved in *The Christmas Journey* have someone to oversee the whole event, to take responsibility for the smooth running of things and to delegate and troubleshoot where necessary. As the Frodsham journey was the inspiration and vision of two people, a shared leadership has worked well.
- Layout and logistical planning team: The layout is dependent on the premises and the creative use of facilities available. A small team can discuss ideas and plan the sequence and smooth transition between rooms.
- Costume and props providers: A list of costumes and props required for the scenes can be circulated in the church. This can bring surprising results: people who are reluctant to work with children or take leading roles can often offer sewing skills or supply items to be used for props.
- Scenery makers: However simple or complicated the scenery is to be, a certain amount of preparation and design are needed before the event. On pages 54–95, the scenes are described in detail so it should be possible for a small group to prepare scenery in advance of the set-up.
- Craft purchasers: Craft materials need to be purchased and items assembled, such as glue sticks, felt-tipped pens and card, so that they are ready for children to use.
- Administrators: Invitations need to be sent out to schools, and transport needs to be booked, if the church is providing it. A

sample invitation is given on page 46. Prayer cards need to be produced (see page 38) and T-shirts ordered if required.

- **Publicity officers:** If the general public are to be invited, there will need to be posters, adverts and publicity in schools and churches.

Helpers needed during the event

- **Leader/organizer(s):** As mentioned before, the overall leadership role can be shared. Although this may seem strange, it is better for the leader or leaders not to have a prime role in the actual event. This releases them to be available if there are any problems with schools, buses, props and other issues. It also means that they are able to chat to teachers and monitor timings to ensure the smooth running of *The Christmas Journey*. The leaders will know most about all aspects of the journey so they will be the best troubleshooters.
- **Journey guides:** With two groups travelling at staggered times, at least two journey guides are needed. They are the people who will lead the children around *The Christmas Journey*, linking the scenes together and encouraging the group to participate in the story. It is best if they have experience of working with children, are able to speak clearly and with confidence, and are not easily flustered if things don't always go according to plan.
- **Journey guides' assistants:** Each group should have at least one or two assistants to organize the children, help with costumes, props and so on and, very importantly, to leave each scene ready for the next group by replacing items in their original locations.
- **Storyteller:** The storyteller meets the children twice, first at the beginning and again at the end of the journey. These scenes are key parts of the journey so it is important that the storyteller is able to learn the scripts and tell the story with empathy and skill. The storytelling is designed in such a way that the storyteller uses an unfolding series of small objects, which give the children a visual focus, enabling them to immerse themselves in the story. It is important for the storyteller to use the open-ended questions at

the end of the storytelling to prompt the children to wonder why Jesus was born. While it would be possible to use two storytellers (one at the beginning, another at the end), using just one gives a better sense of continuity, which is very important. The children are told that they are on a quest to find out what God's rescue plan for the world is, and that the storyteller will meet them at the end to hear what they have discovered. A second storyteller could be used for the second group, although there is time allowed for one person to speak to both groups.

- **Puppeteers**: The stable scene should be prerecorded on to CD. Three or four people are needed to work the puppets, which mime to the script. If numbers allow, a rota for this task saves tired arms! It is important to practise beforehand with the script in order for puppet characters to react in the correct way.
- **Craft helpers**: Several team members are needed to assist the children in making their crafts and also to chat with them and help them to feel at home. These helpers need to prepare tables and ensure that each school receives the correctly labelled items when they go back to school. If there is a display or reading corner for the children to use when crafts are completed, there are more opportunities for conversation.
- **Refreshment team**: Providing refreshments for accompanying adults is an important part of *The Christmas Journey*. While the children are occupied in making the craft, teachers can be offered a comfy place to sit in sight of the children, but in a separate area of the room, with good-quality resources to browse. Helpers can offer tea and coffee with mince pies or biscuits. This is a valuable opportunity for building good relationships with the school staff. Team members will also appreciate refreshments when they have a break between their tasks.
- **Technical support team**: There is some technology involved in *The Christmas Journey*, requiring someone responsible for switching on lights, DVDs and CDs at appropriate times. The CDs can often be operated by people who have other roles in the

scene, such as puppeteers in the stable. Mary can be behind the scenery to look after the music needed in the shepherds' scene.
* 'Gatekeepers', meeters and greeters: It is important that there is always someone around to make sure no child leaves the building during school visits. If a new school group arrives before the previous one has left, there needs to be someone who can explain what to do and make the new school feel welcome. Coats need to be in place for children who are leaving, and timings need to be coordinated. Having a couple of people responsible for these scenarios is very important.

Team training

In order to encourage a friendly and welcoming attitude to the visitors, the *Christmas Journey* team may find the following guidelines helpful. It is useful, when building a team, to incorporate the issues highlighted below into a training session for helpers. Team members will have the opportunity to ask questions about issues that concern them and a code of conduct can be agreed. It is important that the team recognizes the leadership structure and knows whom to approach if they have suggestions or problems. Leaders should be able to give an account of their actions but also to affirm their team. The training session should include an overview of the event, discussion of scenes in detail and ideas for talking to children. It is useful for helpers to have an idea of the 'big picture', to understand where their part fits into the whole and that there may be sound reasons for doing something in a particular way.

It is important for the team to be aware of child protection issues, although there should be no need for helpers to be alone with a child, as groups will be accompanied by school staff. However, it is highly desirable that each helper is CRB-checked. The current UK Government policy is clearly explained by the Churches Child Protection Advisory Service (CCPAS). For more information, visit www.ccpas.co.uk. CCPAS provide invaluable advice and practical help to churches about child protection issues. Good practice guidelines must be understood and followed by team members. Appropriate behaviour when helping children should be discussed in team training. For example, care must be taken, when working closely alongside the children, not to use inappropriate touch. Adults who are not used to working with children in a professional capacity sometimes cannot see the harm in putting an arm around a child or accompanying a child alone to the toilet. As a church, however, we need to show teachers and parents that we not only understand and uphold the law of the land but support the reasoning behind it.

It is also important that helpers are aware that this is not an opportunity to attempt to convert children to Christianity. The story is being offered to the children and adults to help them to reflect upon the real meaning of Christmas and the reason why Jesus was born. The prayer is that seeds will be sown, which will take root, but it is still part of an educational experience for the children and teachers. The locally agreed syllabus requires that children know the facts about the story of the first Christmas and be able to respond to it. They are encouraged to wonder about creation and Jesus' life and death, but not to make a decision about their personal faith. Many children will be from homes where even the Christmas story is not familiar, and some may be of other faiths. Sensitivity is vital in order to develop and maintain trust between the Christian community and the schools.

Encourage the team to focus on what is happening all the time. Even if they don't have a major role in an activity, such as when the children are singing or making crafts, explain to them that it is important to be joining in with the children rather than chatting or getting on with other preparation. If adult helpers are seen to be involved at all times with the children, it encourages the accompanying staff to participate in the journey.

A training day sample outline

Time	Activity
10.00am	Welcome, introductions and opportunity for prayer and worship
10.30am	Outline of the journey: the big picture
11.15am	Coffee
11.30am	Team-building task, such as working on a logo together or designing a craft in groups
12.30pm	Lunch
1.30pm	Guidelines and questions about working with children. Discussion of child protection issues and the importance of referring any problem to the leader(s). Guidelines about sensitivity when working with children and the importance of not proselytizing.
2.15pm	Tea
2.30pm	Work through the first and last scenes with the team, using a storyteller. Ask the questions in the scripts. Encourage the team to think of open-ended questions to use with the children.
3.30–4.00pm	Time of personal reflection and prayer for the event

Budget

It is difficult to be accurate about the amount of money required to put on *The Christmas Journey*. If your church has an outreach budget, it is worth remembering that the event will bring in a huge number of people who will all hear the story of Jesus. Costs will vary depending on the scale of the project and the materials used, but an important consideration is that most costs will be 'one off', so, if you are planning it as an annual event, the overall cost will drop significantly in subsequent years. Setting up the Frodsham *Christmas Journey* cost approximately £500 for the materials, including gazebos, fabrics, corrugated card, paint and timber. For the first couple of years, cheap T-shirts with iron-on computer-generated logos were used for the team. Later, when *The Christmas Journey* became an annual event, professionally printed polo shirts were ordered. There are costs for craft materials, refreshments, booklets and publicity. (If ordered from Lifewords at www.sgmlifewords.com/uk, the booklets are free, but, in the case of *The Christmas Journey* in Frodsham, an equivalent donation to counteract the cost was sent.)

If the church can offer coach transport to and from the event, this is very helpful for schools at a busy time of the year. It is worth asking local councils or businesses for help towards costs, or even to offer to hire a coach and split the cost between the participating schools. This will be cheaper and will make the experience more pleasurable for the staff. It also allows more control over the arrival and departure of children.

Often, the costs are met by individual gifts, although it is important to keep track of the money spent so that, if someone different takes over the running of the event in a subsequent year, they will be able to give the church a good understanding of the budget required. If money is a problem, it should not be a barrier to running a successful event, as many of the items can be borrowed and adapted. A little creativity goes a long way!

Dates and times

A major consideration, when planning your event, is the number of days you are realistically able to commit to *The Christmas Journey*. This will depend on the size of your team, availability of the premises, the number of schools you would like to invite and so on. *The Christmas*

Journey at Frodsham began with three days and progressed to four days as more schools heard about the presentation and wanted an invitation. A larger team could share the workload, enabling more sessions to be offered.

The Christmas Journey is ideally presented as near to the beginning of December as possible. If it is left much later, schools are involved in their own Christmas productions and are reluctant to have children missing from rehearsals. Staff can use the event to stimulate discussion and learning in the lead-up to Christmas.

Organizing the event near the beginning of December also means that, from a personal perspective, the team members are not yet involved in their own Christmas preparations. It is also an ideal opportunity to invite staff, children and their families to Christmas events at the church and in the local Christian community.

If the event is to take place at the beginning of December, detailed planning should begin in September—although it would be wise to inform the church or *Churches Together* team of your thoughts even earlier, so that prayer and dates can be factored into the church calendar.

It is worth investigating other local events and linking *The Christmas Journey* to them if possible. A town Christmas festival or similar event is an ideal opportunity to offer an attraction to the public on behalf of the local churches. Christmas is, of course, a Christian festival, so the journey sits alongside more secular activities quite happily and may bring members of the public into church in a non-threatening way. If the church is seen as taking part in a community event, there could be benefits in publicity and funding, if available. Volunteering to be involved in the planning and preparation of such community projects can build trust and credibility with the general public and is worth pursuing if time allows.

The venue

The way in which *The Christmas Journey* is created depends on the size and layout of your venue. The main presentation area should be divided into five or six separate storytelling rooms (described in detail on pages 54–95). A suggested plan of the storytelling rooms can be found on page 96. It is helpful if the craft area is in a different part of the building from the actual experience. For example, if you are using the worship area for *The Christmas Journey*, then an adjacent church hall is ideal for the craft activity (although it may be necessary for you to adapt the first part to suit your circumstances). Also, a holding area is useful for groups arriving early. Toilets and emergency exits should be clearly labelled and children and adults need to know what fire safety procedures are in place.

Branding and logos

The idea of branding and using logos may be unfamiliar to some members of the church family, but it can make the event more cohesive and professional in nature. Children nowadays are used to sophisticated marketing, so choosing a logo and using it in all publications and information and even on helpers' T-shirts can help to create a sense of belonging and identity for both the team and the participants. If you decide to give children a booklet or pamphlet to take home, it is good to use an image linked to this.

Lifewords (www.sgmlifewords.com) and other publishers produce appropriate literature for Christmas and they will often provide free downloads of the images for PowerPoint presentations and publicity. There may be someone in the church who is experienced in this field and can create the logo and advise on its use. Downloads of clip-art from the Internet could be another avenue to explore. T-shirts can be branded using iron-on computer-generated images. If the budget is small, badges are easy to produce. You could even use sticky labels on a coloured shirt, with the colour agreed between the team beforehand. T-shirts can later be printed professionally if the presentation becomes an annual event. *The Christmas Journey* website (www.christmasjourney.org.uk) provides downloads and links to useful resources for branding.

Dealing with the public

Although *The Christmas Journey* is primarily designed for use with school children, it is possible to open the event to the public. Often, children will be anxious to have the opportunity to bring parents and siblings back to take part in the journey themselves. Extending the event to encompass weekend or evening opening will provide the public with an opportunity to take part in the experience. It may be worth introducing a ticketing system to limit numbers. Remember, too, that children taking part in *The Christmas Journey* during the open sessions need to be accompanied by a responsible adult at all times. Journey guides will need to adapt their presentation of the scenes in order to allow for a wider age range. It could still be possible to send two groups round as in the school version, although it is not necessary to provide a craft activity unless there are plenty of willing helpers. Refreshments can be served and a friendly atmosphere created—again, useful as a means of outreach into the community. It is important that helpers are aware of numbers entering and exiting the building to ensure a smooth flow of visitors.

Encouragement and prayer

It is good to begin each day of *The Christmas Journey* with a short time of prayer together before getting on with practical tasks, so that each team member is affirmed and able to reflect upon the reason for the event. Completing the event with a time of prayer and worship can also be very worthwhile. However, *The Christmas Journey* must be surrounded in prayer from the earliest preparation through to the event and afterwards. There may be local groups who pray specifically for schools, as well as church prayer groups, and it is good to keep them informed of needs and progress. Encouraging the church family to pray for specific needs can help to create ownership and a feeling of being part of the excitement of the event. Regular updates, either by email or in person, are valuable. Prayer cards that use the branding and perhaps a significant Bible verse are useful to hand out at local churches and Christian events. These are likely to be in the public domain, so care should be taken about personal details and wording. The example below is also available on the website.

Please pray for *The Christmas Journey*

On: _____

At: _____

- For the schools invited...
- For the public...
- For the team...
- For safety and enjoyment...
- For all who hear the message of Christmas...
- That God will be glorified!

'I will use stories to speak my message and to explain things that have been hidden since the creation of the world'
(Matthew 13:35).

---

*

Preparing for the event: the local primary schools

Contacting schools

Many churches already have a good relationship with their local primary schools. Building such links is vital, not just in order to bring children into the church but also to offer genuine assistance to hard-pressed staff. Members of your congregation may already serve as school governors, or help with reading, sport or assemblies where appropriate. Creating these opportunities leads to a mutual respect and trust between the church and school. Groups set up to pray for schools can offer confidential prayer, and groups from churches are often involved in running after-school or lunch-time clubs.

It is important to be sensitive to the educational needs and aims of the school. It would be sad if years of prayer and careful nurturing of relationships were spoiled by an overenthusiastic confessional approach. If a relationship of trust is built up, then an invitation to *The Christmas Journey* will probably be very well received and appreciated. A friendly head teacher is a great asset in publicizing your event. Local schools often operate a cluster system, so having a good relationship with one school may lead to recommendations to others. It is worth taking time to research this.

Invitations should be sent out before the October half term. Schools plan their curriculum well in advance—especially for the Christmas period. It is best to allocate a particular slot to each school rather than giving them a choice. The school will soon ask to swap if their session is at an inconvenient time. If coach transport is offered, make pick-up and return times clear to the school, as this allows more control over the arrival and departure of children. It is useful to ask the coach company for a driver's mobile number just in case there are any hitches on the day.

Guidelines for schools

It is important that churches are aware of the needs of the primary school in relation to the School Standards scheme of work and the locally agreed RE syllabus. This may vary from local authority to local authority but all will encompass a programme of study that is broadly Christian. The birth and life of Jesus will undoubtedly be part of that programme and it is worth looking at a copy so that you can demonstrate to the school that the presentation is relevant and useful in delivering the curriculum. Most schools will be very grateful for the offer of the event but, if the area includes a variety of faith groups, the schools will need to know what is going to be covered. They may need to contact parents in order to reassure them that the story is part of the programme of study.

As always when dealing with schools, sensitivity is vital. Some team members may feel that this is an opportunity to evangelize but a school event is not the correct platform for doing so. Unlike the children who attend holiday clubs or lunch-time clubs, these children are not choosing to come to the experience; they are being brought as a class activity. It is important to keep a good relationship with the schools, so a professional approach to the material is an excellent witness, showing that the church recognizes the needs of the pupils. Many churches or Christian groups will include primary school teachers and advice from them would be helpful. For further information about the locally agreed syllabus, contact the Education Office or RE adviser. The Standards Site, www.standards.dfes.gov. uk, is useful for referencing topics likely to be in the school's scheme of work. For example, Attainment Target 2, level 2, expects children to 'realize that some questions that cause people to wonder are difficult to answer', which fits very well with the beginning and end scenes of *The Christmas Journey*. Unit 1c, 'Why do Christians give gifts at Christmas?', ties in well with the wise men scene, and there are several more appropriate links.

If funding allows, a small gift to each school, such as an assembly book, together with publicity material from reputable Christian publishers, is a tangible souvenir of the journey experience. (See resources section on page 116.)

Learning outcomes

By the end of *The Christmas Journey*, most children will be able to:

- Identify some of the significant parts of the Christmas story.
- Place the story in the context of Jesus' life and work.
- Ask questions about why Jesus was born.
- Make connections with the themes in the story and some of the core beliefs of Christianity.

Considering learning styles

When developing *The Christmas Journey*, much thought was given to the varied learning styles of children. It is now widely acknowledged that children learn in different ways. Some children prefer the experiential hands-on approach; others will appreciate storytelling; yet more will respond to entering into the life of a character and acting out a story. *The Christmas Journey* is designed to appeal to the five senses so that there is inclusion for all. Children are also asked to reflect on and wonder about the things they hear and see. Open-ended questions are important to help children to consider their thoughts and feelings. The scripts give suggestions and ideas, particularly for the first and final scenes. Further information about mind-friendly learning and learning intelligences is widely available on the Internet.

Health and safety

Health and safety issues should always be considered (for example, allergies or food intolerances when asking children to taste bread, or the effect of flashing lights, if used, and the safety of electrical equipment in proximity to the visitors). Numbers should be monitored so that there are not too many visitors in each storytelling room. The management of children and adults leaving the building is just as important as when welcoming them. A leader should make sure each group has all the coats, books and craft materials that they are expecting, so that the whole experience is pleasant from beginning to end. As the children relate to their leader, the assigned guide should be aware that it is part of their responsibility to ensure continuity.

Risk assessment

Many schools are now much more regulated about how children can be taken out of school. They need consent forms from parents or carers and will want to know more about the experience in which their children will be involved. A risk assessment needs to be done before each educational visit made by schools and, if the venue can provide a ready-made assessment for the experience, it will be helpful for the teacher organizing the trip. This is not as onerous as it sounds. A sample is given on pages 48–49, although it would need to be tailored to be appropriate for an individual building.

Children with special needs

Children with special needs can benefit greatly from the multi-sensory approach to the story and it can be an amazing and rewarding experience to lead such a group round *The Christmas Journey*. Their responses may be very individual, depending on their level of understanding, but teachers greatly value the event for their children. Helpers need to be sensitive to such groups, and guides may need to adapt to the needs of pupils. Most special schools bring small groups with plenty of helpers trained in looking after the pupils, and their responses can be profound. However, in the case of children with special needs, it may be better to dispense with the craft activity in order to provide more time for the journey itself.

*

Checklist

Three months to go

- Pray. Make prayer cards.
- Decide on the format and leadership structure.
- If necessary, establish a working budget with the church treasurer. If the event is a joint effort, organizations such as *Churches Together* could be approached to assist.

Two months to go

- Assemble the team.
- Send publicity for the event to other churches.
- Send invitations to schools and arrange timetable.
- Book transport if required. Send an itinerary to the coach firm as soon as it has been confirmed.

One month or less to go

- Organize team training.
- Allocate roles.
- Prepare the scenery, puppets, props, costumes and audio resources.
- Organize the craft activity.
- Set up the venue.
- Ensure that toilets are clearly labelled.
- Install lighting and video projection (if appropriate).
- Distribute labels, T-shirts or other 'uniform' items to the team.

- Carry out a risk assessment. Make sure that fire exits are clearly labelled.
- Walk through the experience for the whole team, with the characters in place, so that everyone is familiar with the format.

During the event

- Pray at the beginning of each day.
- Confirm transport arrangements each morning (if possible, take coach driver's phone number).
- Make sure each of the team members is in place. As mentioned, it is better that the team leader is not heavily involved with the presentation so that he or she is free to troubleshoot, network with staff and keep a general overview of timing and organization.
- Make sure everyone knows who is in charge in case of an emergency and that procedures are in place to deal with it.
- Have a system for welcoming school parties, leaving coats, visiting toilets and so on.
- Provide refreshments for staff.
- Provide resources for staff to look through if available. Barnabas promotional material and publications can be easily obtained (see page 116 for details).
- Have a system for ensuring that, on leaving, each group receives their own crafts, books and so on.
- Enjoy the journey! You are sowing seeds that will grow and mature for God's kingdom.

Sample invitation

[Address of hosting church]
[date]

Dear [name of head teacher]

The churches of [name of town] would like to invite the children of [name of school] to take part in a presentation of *The Christmas Journey*. This will be a free multimedia event involving drama, puppets, music, song, crafts and storytelling.

Children will visit six scenes from the story in order to experience the nativity and its relevance today. *The Christmas Journey* will last for approximately one hour and is offered to your Year Two children. The event is planned to take place annually, so younger children will have the opportunity to attend next year. The event can take up to 30 children plus accompanying adults and the churches of [name of town] and [name of sponsor] have kindly agreed to provide coach transport from your school to and from the event. The event will take place at [venue] on [date] and [date] to coincide with [related event if appropriate].

Older and younger children will have the chance to visit the event with their families on [date] from [time] onwards. We would be grateful if you could advertise this in your school newsletters. A flier will be sent separately.

We do hope that your children will be happy to take part at the time offered below. Please could you let us know as soon as possible if this is not convenient so that we can either change your time or invite other schools.

Date: Pick up time: Return time:

We will contact you by telephone before the event to confirm arrangements.

With best wishes

[Name of leader(s)]
[Contact telephone number(s)]
[Contact email address(es)]

Sample risk assessment form

Activity	Hazard	Who is at risk?	Level of risk			Control measures to be taken to reduce risk level to low Severity: S=1–4 (1=low); Likelihood: L=1–4; Risk: R=SxL	Controlled level of risk		
			S	L	R		S	L	R
The Christmas Journey experience	Slips, trips and falls	All	1	2	2	Nobody may run around. Care to be taken when moving around the building. Adequate supervision of visitors to *The Christmas Journey* by teachers and adults.	1	1	1
	Fire	All	1	2	2	No smoking allowed in the building. Sources of ignition must be kept under control. Hot objects must be supervised adequately (such as bulbs, lamps, bread-making equipment). Fire exits to be left clear and unobstructed.	1	1	1
	Electrical equipment	All	1	2	2	All electrical equipment to be electrically tested. Equipment used to be periodically checked during *The Christmas Journey*. Cabling to be routed away from high-risk areas and covered with duct tape.	1	1	1

Sample risk assessment form

Activity	Who				Control measures			
Evacuation of building	All	1	3	3	Use of appropriate exits to be observed at all times. Fire exits to be left clear and unobstructed. In the event of evacuation, everyone to report to the car park for checking. Adequate supervision of visitors to make sure all are evacuated from building calmly and quietly and moved to a place of safety. In event of emergency help being needed, Main Street leaders to contact 999 by mobile phone.	1	2	2
Unloading and loading of buses	Pupils and school staff	2	3	6	Adequate supervision of pupils by teachers and other adults.	1	2	2
Trapping fingers in doors	All	2	2	4	Adequate supervision by teachers and other adults. Pupils given warning about the doors.	1	2	2
Craft activities	Pupils	2	2	4	Adequate supervision by adults and warnings given about using tools safely.	1	2	2

Compiled by [name of compiler] [date]

★

Creating the journey

As we have seen, in travelling *The Christmas Journey*, groups are led around four scenes from the biblical nativity story, after an introduction based on the story of creation. A final scene links the story with Jesus' life, death and resurrection. The whole picture is based on God's rescue plan for the world. The participants are guided through each scene by a leader and at least one assistant. The children meet characters and storytellers in each scene, and leaders are trained to link the characters together.

The six scenes are:

- In the beginning
- Mary's kitchen
- A hillside near Bethlehem
- The stable
- The wise men's palace
- The new beginning

Christmas is a time when people recall the story they learned when young and have shared with their own children, but they may never have related it to the bigger picture and seen its place in the whole story of Jesus' life, death and resurrection. *The Christmas Journey* seeks to remedy this in an interactive way. Each scene is chosen to reflect both its place in the big picture and in the everyday situations that became so extraordinary when God stepped in. For example, Mary is found baking bread when the angel arrives to tell her the news. Leaders encourage their groups to reflect upon the surprise and obedience of Mary as she responds to the astonishing occurrence.

The set

Sets and props can be as simple or elaborate as desired, depending on the skills and talents available. Much will depend, too, on the facilities and amount of space in the building. The church in Frodsham is fortunate to have a square worship area that can be completely cleared of furniture, to accommodate four square, pop-up, dark green gazebos, which act as the storytelling rooms for the four-part nativity story. It is worth buying or borrowing good-quality metal gazebos if you plan to repeat the event, as the plastic ones are more complicated to erect and less robust for attaching drapes.

The gazebos are placed in the corners of the hall, leaving a central uncluttered area in which to tell the first part of the story. Each gazebo is positioned slightly away from the walls to allow extra space for props and, in some cases, to make the storytelling room larger.

Gazebos are ideal for the event as they are easy to assemble, take little room for storage afterwards and can be used creatively by removing or adding sides, drapes and hangings. It may be necessary to try to soundproof some of the walls with blankets, although often it is the adults who notice outside noise, rather than the children, who are used to working in a noisy environment.

If your space is large or has fixed furniture, however, it may be possible to create smaller areas by using screens, wood or even corrugated card. Imaginative use of fabric and lighting can hide a multitude of distractions. Large quantities of dark fabric can be purchased very cheaply from discount textile warehouses, curtain shops and so on. It is worth trying to obtain fabric that will not fray or need ironing so that it can be easily cut and reused.

Creating an enclosed passage system between the gazebos with dark fabric helps to provide a smooth transition from room to room. This keeps the children focused on the story and generates a sense of mystery and expectation. You can link the gazebos together using dark fabric draped over poles or stapled to slats of wood. Take care that the wood is secured safely to the gazebo in order to prevent accidents. Strong string can be used to fix the wood securely. You should ask the children to take care when moving around. The nature of the journey is such that children are rarely distracted and respond very positively to moving from room to room in a mysterious and anticipatory manner.

The room plan for *The Christmas Journey* in Frodsham is shown on page 96 and on the website. Photographs of *The Christmas Journey* in Frodsham can also be accessed on the website.

Lighting

Lighting plays a vital role in creating an intimate atmosphere in each setting. It is easy to create a professional effect with simple lighting readily found in local furniture and DIY stores. Clip-on spotlights, free-standing uplighters and strings of Christmas lights can all be used to good effect. Obviously, care needs to be taken with hiding wires and adapters. Photos and diagrams on the website show the set-up used in Frodsham, but much will depend on the arrangement of electrical sockets in your building. Although the rooms should be as dark as possible, attention to health and safety is paramount and, for this reason, background lighting is advisable.

Part Two

★

Scene 1

In the beginning

—————————— Bible background ——————————
Genesis 1:1—2:4 and 3:1-6

Aim

To introduce the idea that Christians believe that God created the
world as a beautiful and special place, but that people have gone
their own way, breaking their relationship with God and spoiling
much of God's handiwork by being selfish. God needed to rescue
his world and his people.

Setting the scene

This scene is designed to put the whole story into context. God
created a perfect world for people to live in and care for, but people
have misused their privilege of being put in charge of the world to
spoil both the environment and their relationship with God. The
Old Testament tells of the people's struggle to repair this relationship
by keeping the law—which proved impossible. God's only option
was for his Son, Jesus, to show people how to live and ultimately to
pay the price for the hurt world and its people. *The Christmas Journey*
develops in such a way that the children are asked to wonder how
God is going to mend and heal the problems of the world through
the things that they see and hear.

Characters

• Storyteller

Scenery

A plain, uncluttered space with little to distract from the story. There should be subdued lighting and a quiet atmosphere.

Props

- One piece of black felt measuring approximately 60cm x 10cm and rolled up in preparation for the story.
- Seven 8cm squares of felt in the following colours: two plain yellow; two plain green; one light blue with a dark blue curve across the middle; one light blue with a dark blue triangle laid diagonally across it, dividing it in two; one yellow with a black triangle laid diagonally across it, dividing it in two.
- Four small gift boxes, each slightly different so that they are easy to identify. These boxes correspond to a part of the story and are carefully revealed as that part is reached. The boxes need to contain further items, as follows:
  * Box 1: a small fabric leaf and some small artificial flowers.
  * Box 2: a small sun made of gold card, a smaller moon made of silver card and some small silver confetti stars.
  * Box 3: small model fish and birds (either plastic ones from the Early Learning Centre or wooden ones from a craft shop).
  * Box 4: wooden animals (for example, from a Noah's ark set) or plastic ones from the Early Learning Centre, and two small people figures (preferably made of wood).
- Small pieces of grey felt.
- An uneven circle of greaseproof paper.
- A wooden tray, large enough to hold all of the above items.

Pile the seven felt squares in the correct colour order with the first colour on top (see script). Place the felt squares, the rolled black felt, the filled gift boxes on the tray, the small pieces of grey felt and the greaseproof paper on the tray.

You will also need:

- A DVD of stars, planets and so on projected on to the ceiling or a wall behind the storyteller.
- Quiet music playing in the background, such as 'Becoming Still' by Simeon Wood (CD: *Celtic Heart*; see www.simeonwood.com).

The journey

The children assemble outside the first space and are told that they are going on a special journey. The leaders build up a sense of wonder and quiet anticipation as the children wait to enter the room. They are asked to enter quietly—perhaps through a starlit doorway—and look around them. As they come in, there are images of creation to observe, which are projected on to the ceiling or a wall, along with appropriate music to set the scene. The storyteller is already in place, sitting on the floor, with the tray within easy reach. He or she welcomes the children and asks them to sit quietly around the carpet. The storyteller draws attention to the beauty of the images. The images cease and the music slowly fades.

The storyteller asks the children if they are looking forward to Christmas… and what presents they are hoping for. He or she then asks them what is the biggest present that they have ever received. Allow the children to give a variety of answers, expressing appropriate appreciation of these presents. This leads into the story…

NB: Don't rush the storytelling, and try to focus on the visuals you are presenting, not on the children.

Script: In the beginning

Storyteller: These are all big presents. They are wonderful presents. Yes, yes. That's a big present, too.

But, do you know that there are some presents that are so big that nobody notices them? They are so huge that they are really hard to see. The only way to see these presents is to go right back to when they were given... right back to the beginning.

In the beginning... in the beginning when God created the heavens and the earth...

... there was...

Slowly unroll the first 10cm of black felt. Unroll it from your right to your left (so that the children will read the story left to right).

... nothing!

The earth was barren, with no form of life; it was under a roaring ocean covered in darkness.

But the Spirit of God was moving over the water.

Allow your hand to hover over the unrolled part of the felt.

Then God said, 'I command light to shine!' And light started shining.

Show the top square (a plain yellow square) and place it on the black felt, at the far right-hand side.

> This light was the light of life. It was the light of God shining in the dark of the world. It was the light that all light comes from.

> God looked at the light and saw that it was good. He separated light from darkness, and named the light 'Day' and the darkness 'Night'.

Hold one hand, as if in blessing, above the yellow square. Then encourage the children to give a thumbs-up sign as you say, 'It is good!'

> Evening came and then morning—that was the first day.

> Then God said, 'I command a dome to separate the water above it from the water below it.' And that is what happened.

Show the blue square with the darker blue curve across its middle, and put it down on the black felt, next to the yellow square.

> God made the dome, and named it 'Sky'.

Place a hand of blessing above the blue square and encourage the thumbs-up sign, as before.

> Evening came and then morning—that was the second day.

And then God said, 'I command the water under the sky to come together in one place, so there will be dry ground.' And that is what happened.

Show a green felt square and carefully put it down in line next to the blue square.

God named the dry ground 'Land', and he named the water 'Sea'. God looked at what he had done and he saw that it was good.

Then God said, 'I command the earth to produce all kinds of plants, including fruit, trees and grain.' And that is what happened.

Take the box containing the leaf and flowers, open it and place the items on the green felt square.

God looked at what he had done and saw that it was good.

Place a hand of blessing above the green square and encourage the thumbs-up sign, as before.

Evening came and then morning—that was the third day.

And then God said, 'I command lights to appear in the sky, to separate day from night and to show the time for seasons, special days and years. They will shine in the sky to give light to the earth.' And that is what happened.

Show the felt square divided into one yellow and one black triangle, and slowly place it next to the green square.

> God made two powerful lights, the brighter one to rule the day…

Take the box containing the sun, moon and stars, open it and place the sun on the yellow triangle of felt.

> … and a lesser one to rule the night.

Place a white moon on the black triangle of felt.

> He also made the stars.

Scatter the stars around the moon on the black triangle.

> He placed the lights in the sky to shine on the earth, to rule the day and the night, and to separate light from darkness. And God looked at what he had done and saw that it was good.

Place a hand of blessing above the yellow and black square and encourage the thumbs-up sign, as before.

> Evening came and then morning—that was the fourth day.

> And then God said, 'I command the sea to be full of living creatures, and birds to fly in the air.' And that's what happened.

Show the felt square divided into a light blue and a dark blue triangle, and place it next to the yellow and black square.

> God looked at what he had done and saw that it was good. He gave the living creatures his blessing— he told the sea creatures to live everywhere in the sea...

Take the box containing the fish and birds, open it and place some little fish on the dark blue triangle of felt. Ask the children for suggestions of other creatures that swim.

> ... and countless birds, in every colour and size, to live everywhere on earth.

Place some little birds on the light blue triangle of felt and ask children for suggestions of different types of bird or other creatures that fly.

> Evening came and then morning—that was the fifth day.

> And then God said, 'I command the earth to give life to all kinds of tame animals, wild animals and reptiles.' And that is what happened.

Show the second green felt square and place it next to the light and dark blue square. Take the box containing the animals, open it and place two animals on the square.

God made living creatures to run and jump and skip and hop and creep and crawl in every corner of the world. He looked at what he had done and saw that it was good.

Place a hand of blessing above the green square and encourage the thumbs-up sign, as before.

And then God said, 'Now we will make humans; they will be like us. We will let them rule the fish, the birds and all other living creatures.' So God created humans to be like himself.

Place a couple of small wooden people into the palm of your hand.

He made people and breathed his life into each one of them.

Breathe into your closed palms and then place the models on to the green felt square among the animals.

God gave them his blessing and said, 'Have lots of children!'

Hold your hand over the model in a sign of blessing.

God said, 'Fill the earth with people and look after the land. Take care of the fish in the sea, the birds in the sky and every animal on the earth. I have provided all kinds of fruit and grain for you to eat.

And I have given green plants as food for everything else that breathes.'

God looked at what he had done. All of it was very good!

Sweep your hand over the whole cloth in a sign of blessing. Encourage the thumbs-up sign as before.

Evening came and then morning—that was the sixth day.

So the heavens and the earth and everything else was created. By the seventh day, God had finished his work. God blessed the seventh day and made it special, because on that day he rested from his work.

Place the final yellow square on the black felt. Pause.

On this day, people go to different places to remember the great presents. Only you know what you would put on this square as your favourite place to remember. It might be in your garden by a tree, in a church, or in your bedroom. It might be in the mountains or by the ocean or a lake. I don't know where your place is. Only you know.

What I do know is that Christians often mark this day with a cross.

Draw an imaginary cross as a bold gesture in the air above the whole story, then sit back and pause awhile.

The storyteller then asks the following three questions, one at a time, allowing children to respond.

> I wonder which part of God's present you like best…
>
> I wonder which part of God's present is the most important part…
>
> I wonder if we can leave out any part of his present and still have all the present we need…

The storyteller now asks the following rhetorical questions, asking the children not to answer but to hold on to their thoughts and to reflect. If children are anxious to speak, ask them to hold on to what they would like to say for the time being.

> I wonder what would happen if people chose to live in darkness rather than light…

Place the people on the edge of the black felt underlay.

> I wonder what would happen if people began to destroy some of the creatures that swim and the birds that fly… and some of the animals and reptiles…

Turn over one fish and one bird, and lay down one animal.

> I wonder what would happen if people destroyed some of the plants and trees…

Turn over the leaf and some of the flowers.

> I wonder what would happen if people messed up the water...

Put small pieces of grey felt on to the second square.

> I wonder what would happen if people filled the air with dirt and pollution...

Put the uneven circle of greaseproof paper over the 'day and night' square.

> I wonder what would happen if people didn't rest and remember all the amazing presents...

Move the seventh square way from the rest and turn it over.

> I wonder what would happen if people turned away from the light that all light comes from...

Dramatically detach the first square from the rest and toss it away to land upside down outside the darkness.

> I wonder what you would do to put right all this mess...

> I wonder what God would do if his present got spoilt...

Pause.

Perhaps you will be able to find out some of the answers as you travel round the journey. I wonder what God will do to begin to mend all that has been spoiled? Will you watch out on the journey and see what God does? I'll see you later and you can tell me what you have discovered…

The storyteller remains in place while leaders quietly ask their group to follow them into the first gazebo.

★

Mary's kitchen

———————— Bible background ————————
Luke 1:26–38 and Matthew 1:18–25

Aim

To help the children to understand that Jesus was a very special baby and that Mary was an ordinary girl who was obedient to God.

Setting the scene

Mary was a young girl who lived in Nazareth. She was engaged to Joseph, a carpenter, and presumably lived the life of an ordinary Jewish girl. Her life was turned upside down when she was visited by the angel Gabriel, who told her that she was going to be the mother of God's own Son.

The Jewish people had been waiting a long time for God to send someone to rescue them—a special person who would come to restore God's kingdom on earth—and Mary would have been aware of the scriptures concerning this promised rescuer. She must have had a tremendous faith to be willing to take on a role that was going to cause embarrassment and shame to both her family and to Joseph. Her belief in God was able to override her fears and she was prepared to trust him to look after her.

Joseph was also visited by an angel and he, too, must have had great faith in order to accept Mary as his wife and Jesus as his child. Here we see a simple young girl accepting God's promises with obedience and joy against all the odds.

Characters

- Mary
- The angel Gabriel

Costume

Traditional eastern dress for Mary; white tunic-type garment for Gabriel over light trousers and a T-shirt.

Scenery

If possible, the inside of a kitchen showing a painted stone wall with a shelf in the style of the times, and dark cloths or screens to two sides of the gazebo.

Props

A small table, a tablecloth, an old-fashioned ceramic mixing bowl, some bread dough, a wooden platter, some bread (cut into cubes), a bread-making machine (hidden behind the scenes).

The journey

The children are led from the previous scene into the first gazebo. Behind the scenes, a bread-making machine has been set up earlier to provide the smell of baking bread. The scenery is simple: a painted wall with shelf of the style of the times. A table holds a mixing bowl with dough for Mary to knead. There is a tablecloth on the table and a wooden platter holding the cubed bread.

The leader encourages the group to sit on the floor and Mary greets them. She tells them she is making bread and explains that she is kneading the dough to help her mother make bread for the family. There is no script for this first part of the scene, although one could be developed if the actor playing Mary is not happy to ad lib. A simple impromptu script would include a welcome to the children, Mary telling the children her name and a little about what she is doing (how the bread is made, the role of flour, yeast and water, why you need to knead dough and so on). She could explain that she has to leave the dough in a warm place to rise before she can bake it in the oven. She offers the children a taste of the prepared bread, and leaders help to pass the platter round. All of these things could be written down, but spontaneity is important so that Mary is genuinely surprised by the entrance of the angel Gabriel.

NB: Leaders should be aware that some children may not want to taste the bread; indeed, some may be allergic to flour or yeast. Teachers who accompany the group should be warned beforehand, although often the children will know themselves what they are allowed to eat. You may find that white bread without 'bits' is often the most popular, even if not authentic.

When the bread has been distributed and all the children have had a chance to taste it, the leader or actor could use some prearranged words to show that Mary is ready to be disturbed (for example, 'Isn't this bread good?'). Mary is surprised by the entrance of the angel Gabriel. Using a simple script, she is told she is going to have a baby and that he will be God's Son. She responds to the angel with surprise and obedience. The angel leaves, followed shortly by Mary, who tells the children she is going to tell her family and Joseph.

Leaders spend a little time exploring Mary's response to the angel (asking the children how they think she felt) and then explain to the children that they are moving forward some months and travelling to Bethlehem where the baby is to be born.

Script: Mary's kitchen

Mary is kneading dough. She welcomes the children into her kitchen, tells them what she is doing (as outlined above), and offers them a piece of bread. The helpers pass the bread to the children. Once the children have tasted the bread, the angel enters, unseen by Mary.

Angel:	Mary, Mary!
Mary:	*(To the audience)* Someone's calling me. *(She turns)* Who are you? What do you want?
Angel:	I am the angel Gabriel, sent by God to give you a message.
Mary:	What? For me? A message for me from God?
Angel:	Yes, Mary. God is going to send his Son into the world, and he's chosen you to be the baby's mother.
Mary:	But how is that going to happen? I'm not even married yet!
Angel:	The Holy Spirit will come to you, and when the baby is born he will be called Jesus.
Mary:	I can hardly believe this is happening to me! I'm so pleased God has chosen me!
Angel:	Nothing is impossible with God!

Gabriel departs to the next room, where he waits behind a screen for his next entrance.

Mary:	I must go quickly and tell Joseph and my family. Goodbye, everyone!

Mary exits in the same direction as Gabriel.

★

A hillside near Bethlehem

——————————— Bible background ———————————
Luke 2:8–20

Aim

To show the children that even ordinary people like the shepherds were able to follow Jesus.

Setting the scene

The shepherds would have been rough men living out in the cold on the hillside, looking after their sheep. They would probably have been uneducated and not respected among the good citizens of Bethlehem, yet God chose them to be the first to know that Jesus had been born. They were so convinced by this message that they left their sheep and went to the town to find the newborn baby. This part of the story shows how much God cares for those who are poor and dispossessed.

Characters

• The angel Gabriel
• Children dressed as shepherds

Scenery

The scenery can be simple. Cut out shapes of hills, glue or staple them to corrugated card and tie them to the side of the gazebo; or paint a scene with the lights of Bethlehem in the distance and fields in the foreground.

Large rolls of corrugated card can be obtained from an educational supplier; alternatively, a shop that sells large white goods often has spare corrugated card packaging. It is worth investigating your Local Education Authority supplier, as churches are often able to register to use these stores and items can be easily purchased at a discount.

For more substantial scenery, a simple timber frame can be made for the card to be stapled to. If used carefully, this is easily dismantled for use in subsequent years. Don't forget to label rolls of card and wooden slats for the next year—it's very easy to forget what you have done.

Poster or emulsion paint is readily available and suitable for the purpose. The painting can be very simple. Collect old Christmas cards showing the hillside and Bethlehem (these are useful to copy). Children's Christmas story books are handy sources for copying simple scenery, too. Trace the image required for the scenery on to an acetate sheet. Then use an OHP to project the image on to scenery panels standing against a wall. The image will be enlarged and the outline can be drawn on to the scenery and then painted.

Christmas lights help to create the illusion of a starry night (the hanging variety are ideal). There should be one bright star shape more obvious than the rest.

Props

- A basket containing tea towels to distribute to children for headdresses. A simple band can be made using decorative shirring elastic tied into a circle.
- Recorded music to herald the entrance of the angel Gabriel, such as the beginning of the 'Messiah' track from the CD *Heatseeker* by Tribe (Warner Resound, 1998).

The journey

The children are led along the covered passage into the second gazebo (see page 96). As they enter the room, the children are encouraged to look around the scene and imagine where they are. They are asked who looks after the sheep... and if they would like to be shepherds. To help with this, they are asked to wear a tea-towel headdress. Helpers are useful here to speed the process of dressing up. Some children may not want to take part, which is fine.

Once the children have put their headdresses on, the leaders ask them to imagine that they are shepherds looking after their sheep on a cold night. Leaders help to create the atmosphere by building up a sense of mystery and slight apprehension, talking about the wild animals and the dark (nothing too scary, but children enjoy a mild sense of danger). At a prearranged signal (for example, 'Isn't it cold here?') a loud piece of music heralds the entrance of the angel Gabriel, who has been hiding behind the scenery. (Mary could operate the music from behind the gazebo, where a CD player is hidden.) Gabriel tells the shepherds not to be afraid, but that a special baby has been born that night in Bethlehem and that they are to leave their sheep and travel to the town to see the child.

Gabriel then exits, in the opposite direction from the one that the children will use, so that he is ready for the next group. Leaders discuss the surprising news with the children and ask them to follow them quietly to the next room. On the way, they quietly sing, 'Where are you going, shepherds?' (see page 97 for details).

Script: The angel Gabriel

Angel: (Appearing from behind a screen) Praise to God in heaven and peace to his people on earth! Don't be afraid, little shepherds. I have brought you good news. God has sent a Saviour into the world. He has been born today in Bethlehem. You will know who he is, because you will find him dressed in baby clothes and lying on a bed of hay.

Praise to God in heaven and peace to his people on earth!

The angel exits through the door by which the shepherds entered.

★

Scene 4

The stable

———————————— Bible background ————————————
Luke 2:5–7

Aim

To help the children understand that Jesus was born in difficult circumstances, yet he was a special baby, visited by both people who were rich and people who were poor.

Setting the scene

In this scene, the animal puppets tell the children what has recently happened in their stable. God didn't choose a palace for the baby to be born in, but a humble stable. Jesus was born into a working-class family in difficult surroundings. He spent his first couple of years as a refugee. He knows what it is like to be an outsider and to live in a foreign land.

Characters

Four large hand puppets: a horse, a sheep, a cow and a donkey. These can be obtained from specialized stores and can be operated by two to four people. Details of suppliers are on the *Christmas Journey* website, www.christmasjourney.org.uk.

Scenery

Dark walls draped with fabric. A half-sized screen of corrugated card is fixed to one wall of the gazebo, painted to look like a timber wall. This is high enough for the puppeteers to sit behind to work the animal puppets. Behind them, more dark fabric is hung.

Lighting should be subdued to create a dark and cosy atmosphere, with spotlights on the animals.

Props

- Models of Mary, Joseph, and a manger in which baby Jesus has been placed. (These are stylized figures approximately 40cm tall, easily made with papier mâché on a wire frame, then painted. There are photographs of the models on the *Christmas Journey* website.)
- Straw and sacks to give a stable effect.
- CD recording of the script so that the puppeteers can mime. (This allows different members of the team to work the puppets when appropriate.)

The journey

Children walk through the passage from the hillside scene (see page 96) and enter the stable, where the animal puppets appear to be resting. The model crib scene is placed to the side of the animal screen. Leaders encourage the children to think about where they might be and make sure that they have noticed the baby lying in the manger, pointing out that this is most unusual. Once the children are seated on the floor, the animals come to life and talk about what they have just experienced in the stable.

The script appeals to both children and adults and lasts for about four and a half minutes. The puppeteers switch on the prerecorded CD when the children are settled and move the puppets as indicated by the script.

Script: The stable

Horse:	Who's this lot coming into our lowly cattle shed now?
Sheep:	Ooooh, I don't know. Probably more visitors to see where a mother laid her baby, in our manger for his bed.
Cow:	Let's have a look. Who have we now? There have been school children and grown-ups, teachers and bus drivers…
Horse:	It was peaceful before, wasn't it?
Donkey:	Aye.
Horse:	Until late last night. We'd all gone to bed and it was nice and peaceful… a silent night. Then the door crashed open and since then it's been like a city centre.
Donkey:	Aye.
Sheep:	The innkeeper's wife brought them in—the girl and her man—brought them to my stall and said they should sleep with me as my stall was the cleanest in the whole stable. (Looks smug)
Horse:	You could tell she was going to have a baby. I could tell straight away.
Sheep:	So they settled down on my clean straw. People in my stall!
Cow:	Yes, then, just when we'd all settled down to go to sleep, the girl started to cry out to the man—desperately crying out that 'her time had come'.
Sheep:	The poor man went running off to get help. The door crashed open again, and help came.

Horse:	The man was no use—just stood there looking worried. Kept saying he knew about carpentry but not about childbirth.
Cow:	Then the baby was born. Didn't he make a noise? Until his mother comforted him. She wrapped him in a cloth and... *(interrupted)*
Sheep:	... used our manger, our food trough, as a cot for the baby.
Cow:	Well, she couldn't have put him on the floor—it was so cold. She had to find somewhere to lay down his sweet head.
Horse:	Then all the helpers left and I hoped we could go back to sleep, but no! It was like there was a new light, a big light, left on over our stable.
Donkey:	Aye.
Horse:	It was dark all around, but there seemed to be light just where we all were. It was strange.

Long pause. All the animals look at horse.

Donkey:	Aye.
Cow:	Then the door burst open again and in came a bunch of shepherds.
Sheep:	I wished they'd brought their sheep with them. I could do with meeting some nice sheep.
Horse:	When they saw the baby in the food trough, wrapped in cloth bands, they were so-o-o-o excited. They said it was a sign. I thought they'd had too much mint tea!
Donkey:	Aye.

Horse: They kept saying a light had appeared in the sky and an angel had told them not to be afraid, and 'this day in King David's home town a Saviour is born for you. He is Christ the Lord.' Then the angel had said the shepherds would know it was true because the baby would have no proper cot and no proper bedclothes, but would be lying in a bed of hay. (*Laughs*) Definitely too much mint tea!

Donkey: Aye.

Cow: Then they said a whole lot of angels appeared, saying, 'Praise God in heaven! Peace on earth to everyone who pleases God.'

Horse: Definitely too much mint tea.

Donkey: Aye.

Pause.

Sheep: I know shepherds look after us sheep, but when they sleep rough on a hillside, in the bleak mid-winter, they smell worse than a dead wolf. Why couldn't the angels have told someone posh?

Cow: Like who?

Sheep: Someone different. Why not... mystical men from the east, who travel on camels, wear rich-coloured clothes and bring exotic gifts... and smell nice?

Horse: Oh, people like that wouldn't believe what they were told, even by an angel. They'd need a sign to follow, something in the sky, like stars. People like that wouldn't come. Some people will never believe what they are told.

Donkey: Aye.

Cow: Then, when the shepherds left, they just couldn't stay quiet or keep still.

Sheep: They must have told everyone what they had seen.

Horse: Yes, since then we've had nothing but people, people, people—children, grown-ups, old and young. I wonder how long people will come seeking for this baby. What did they call him? Jesus?

Donkey: Aye... Jesus!

The puppets return to sleep and the leaders ask the children to move quietly on to the next room.

Scene 5

The wise men's palace

—————————— Bible background ——————————
Based on Matthew 2:1–12

The scene is set as the wise men prepare to leave their homeland to go and find Jesus. The actual story is not told but is based on the imagined thoughts of the men as they pack their bags.

Aim

To help the children to understand that God wanted all kinds of people to seek Jesus, and to explain that the wise men brought unexpected presents for the baby.

Setting the scene

The wise men came from the east (it may have been Persia or Babylon). There is no biblical evidence that there were only three people; this is assumed because three presents are mentioned. The Bible does not say that they were kings, either, but they were obviously from a noble background as the Greek text calls them royal astrologers. They were welcomed into Herod's court, which was an obvious place to go as they believed that they were looking for a newborn king. Their presents had great meaning for Jesus.

This part of the story shows that God sent Jesus not only for Jewish outsiders who lived in poverty, but also for those with power and status outside the Jewish faith.

Characters

- Leader
- Some children dressed as wise men

Scenery

The gazebo is draped with dark cloth and rich fabrics to give the impression of an eastern tent-like palace. (Think Casbah meets Arabian Nights!) Indian saris are ideal and are readily available (see the Internet for suppliers). Sparkly fabrics that catch the light can be obtained cheaply from discount fabric shops. Net curtaining, drapes and remnants can all be used to good effect. A flimsy curtain at the door can give the impression of entering into a different world.

Clip-on spotlights can be positioned to catch the light of the fabric. Red bulbs can create a warm atmosphere. Christmas lights can give an exotic effect.

Props

- A low table covered in an exotic cloth and holding the following items:
  * a gold box, to represent the gift of gold.
  * a glass perfume jar containing a small amount of perfume mixed with olive oil, to represent the gift of frankincense.
  * a small cloth.
  * a screw-top jar containing some hand cream, to represent the gift of myrrh.
  * some pot pourri to create exotic smells (a plug-in cinnamon air freshener will add to the atmosphere).
  * a basket of exotic fruits.
  * some eastern-looking jars.
  * dried grasses, baskets and so on.
  * some boxes of costume jewellery.
- A coat stand holding cloaks, hats and drapes. The hats can be very flamboyant: old hats from charity shops can be dressed up

with chiffon scarves, old jewellery, feathers and so on. Velvet curtains make excellent cloaks.
- An old-fashioned bag to pack the presents in.
- Small toys and clothes suitable for a baby.

Any props that create a feeling of opulence and mystery can be used. **NB:** Frankincense and myrrh can be obtained from aromatherapy outlets, but be aware of allergies if these oils are used.

The journey

The children are led from a dusty, humble stable scene through another dark tunnel into the exotic world of the wise men's eastern palace. The contrast should be dramatic, providing a real 'wow' factor. There are baskets of toys, children's clothes and presents suitable for a baby on the floor. There is a coat stand with hats and cloaks on it.

The leader asks the children where they think they might be. They are invited to sit, knowing that they are in the palace of the wise men. The men are astrologers who have been studying books and watching the stars. They have noticed a new star indicating that an important king has been born. They are preparing to go and find the new baby.

The leader (or teacher) chooses a few of the children (boys and girls) to dress as the wise men in cloaks and hats. (It is often useful for a leader to dress up, too, thus encouraging the children). Once the children are ready, the leader asks the group what kind of things the children would take if they were to visit a new baby. The children are encouraged to find presents such as toys, rattles and clothes and help to pack them in a bag.

The leader then indicates the other gifts on the table. They discuss the fact that these are strange gifts for a new baby. The leader tells the children that gold, the most precious of metals, is fit for a king.

Frankincense is a sweet-smelling incense, which was used when people worshipped God, reminding us that Jesus is God's Son. Myrrh is a fragrant spice used as a soothing ointment. Traditionally, it is thought to represent Jesus' death on the cross. The gifts are given to the three wise men to complete the scene and the children are told that the men set out to see Jesus.

The leader then asks the group if they think that is the end of the story. They are told that they are going 'back to the future' and travelling forward in time to the present day. Costumes are removed and the children move on, singing 'Where are you going, wise men?' (see page 97). The helpers stay to tidy the scene for the next group.

There is no set script for this room because it is interactive, so the leader simply needs to be aware of the aims of the scene and happy to encourage the children to participate. There should be enough toys and gifts to allow every child to join in if they want to. A sample script is given below, although, depending on the reaction of the children, it could be different every time.

Sample script: The wise men's palace

Leader: Where do you think we are? Who do you think lives here?

Allow time for the children to answer and to look round at the surroundings.

We don't know that there were three wise men—there could have been more—it's just that three presents are mentioned in the Bible story. We don't think that the wise men were necessarily kings, but they were important men who studied the stars. One day they saw a new star, which they hadn't noticed before. Their books told them it meant that a special baby king had been born, so they decided to follow the star and go and find the baby.

Now, if they were important men, they probably wore fine clothes. Who would like to dress up as a wise man?

Select two or three children (boys and girls) and help them to put on the cloaks and hats.

If you were going to visit a new baby, what would you take?

Allow the children to make suggestions, then ask them to look for toys and gifts to put in a bag for the baby.

These are all lovely presents to take for a new baby, but the Bible tells us that the wise men took some other gifts, too. Does anyone know what they were?

Allow time for suggestions.

The first gift was gold.

Pick up the 'gold' from the table and give it to one of the wise men to hold.

Gold was a present to show that the new baby was a very important child—probably a king.

The second gift was frankincense.

Pick up the frankincense from the table.

> Frankincense is a precious perfume, which was used in the temple or holy place. It has a lovely smell and helps people to worship God. This shows us that the wise men thought Jesus was special and could be worshipped.

Sprinkle a little of the perfumed oil on to a cloth and pass it round to allow the children to smell it. Give the container to the second wise man. Then pick up the myrrh.

> Myrrh is an ointment used to soothe people when they are sore or hurting. It helps to heal wounds. In hot countries it is sometimes used when people die. It seems a strange present for a baby, doesn't it?

Ask the children to imagine the feel of the soothing properties of the myrrh on their skin. Give the myrrh to the third wise man.

> Once the wise men had their gifts ready, they set out to find Jesus. They travelled a long way over the desert, following the star until they found him. And this is where our story ends... or does it? Do you remember that the very first storyteller told us that he would meet us again at the end? I wonder where he is...

Scene 6

The new beginning

———————— Bible background ————————
Based on John 3:16–21

Aim

To allow the children to reflect upon the things that they have seen and to see Christmas as the beginning of Jesus' life and teaching about God. To understand that the events of the first Christmas fit into the bigger picture of Christian belief about who Jesus was and why he was born.

Setting the scene

This is the part of the journey where the Christmas story is put into context for the children and they are asked to wonder about its relevance to their own lives and the life of the world around them. They hear about Jesus growing up, significant events in his life and the final week before his death. They are told about the cross and the resurrection. They are asked to wonder what all of this is about and are told that they can take the story with them back into their own lives. Using a similar method of storytelling as in the first scene, the story is designed to give a feeling of continuity and resolution to the journey.

Characters

Storyteller (ideally the same person as in the first scene)

Scenery

The scene is set in a modern-day living room, with a plain mat, a small Christmas tree, some wrapped presents, Christmas decorations, Christmas stockings, Christmas cards, some easy chairs, a small television set, an electric fire with a surround (or a card model or painting of a fireplace), some framed pictures, some house plants, and an Advent calendar.

Use table lamps or uplighters to give bright lighting.

Props

- The roll of black felt and the set of seven coloured felt squares used in the first scene (see page 55).
- Six different small gift boxes. The boxes need to contain further items, as follows:
  * Box 1: a small wooden dove shape
  * Box 2: some seeds sealed between two pieces of clear tape, and three small fabric leaves
  * Box 3: a tealight candle and a small box of matches
  * Box 4: some wooden bird shapes and a small wooden boat shape
  * Box 5: a small wooden cross and a small wooden figure of Jesus (with hands stretched out)
  * Box 6: some small wooden people figures.
- A wooden manger and baby (from a nativity set).
- A wooden tray large enough to hold the items listed above.
- A sample of the book to be given later to each child (see www.sgmlifewords.com for ideas).

The journey

The storyteller is already in place in the 'living room', waiting to greet the children. They have met him in the first scene, where he told them the story of creation and asked them to find out about God's great rescue plan for the world. The children are led out from the sumptuous but mysteriously lit eastern palace into the bright, cosy atmosphere of the modern living room. The room is decorated as if for Christmas, with a Christmas tree, decorations and Christmas cards. The mat is in front of the fireplace.

The storyteller welcomes the children and asks them to sit around the mat. The adults can sit in the easy chairs and everyone is encouraged to relax and enjoy the festive scene. The storyteller then asks the children if they have enjoyed the journey and, after some preliminary chat, leads into the final part of the story. During the telling of the story, it is best to encourage the children to reflect quietly rather than to talk.

The children will be familiar with the materials and the storytelling method from the story of creation. The same pattern is used in order to demonstrate the continuity of the story and God's plan to repair our broken world.

Script: The new beginning

Have the black felt for the story rolled out ready. Have the seven felt squares in a pile as before, and the other items in their smaller boxes. Remember that the squares are placed on the black felt starting at your right, so that they unfold left to right for the children.

Storyteller: Did you enjoy the journey?

Allow time for a few answers.

I wonder in what ways you think God's beautiful present has been spoilt… I wonder if you have any ideas from what you have seen about what God was going to do to repair his broken world…

Lift up the wooden manger and baby.

In the beginning—in the second beginning—was…

… a baby. God had chosen Mary to become the mother of his only Son.

Place down the first yellow square and put the manger on it.

This baby was the light for the world. He was the light that all light comes from. Mary and her husband Joseph looked after the baby. The baby grew and became a child… and then an adult. When Jesus was about 30 years old, he went to the River Jordan, where his cousin John was baptizing people.

Place the blue square next to the yellow square.

John baptized Jesus. Jesus went down into water…

Push your hand down into the square and then lift it up again slowly.

… and John lifted him back into the light. Some people nearby said that they saw a dove come down from heaven, close to Jesus.

Remove the dove from its box and slowly place it on the blue square.

Others heard a voice, which said, 'You are my own dear Son, and I am pleased with you.'

Hold a hand in blessing above the blue square.

Now Jesus began his work. But what was his work? His work was to put God's gift back together again—to repair what had been spoilt.

He began by telling stories.

Place the green square next to the blue square.

These stories were like seeds sown, not in the soil but in people's hearts.

Place the seeds along the bottom of the green square, nearest the children.

The seeds grew and helped people to learn more about God's love, more about what God is like, and more about God's great rescue plan to repair his world.

For each of the three things mentioned, place a small leaf above the seeds on the green square.

What else did Jesus do? He challenged the darkness...

Place the yellow and black creation square next to the green square, but with one hand 'pushing' against the black (night) part of the square.

> … and came close to people, especially those whom nobody else came close to. Watch. Look.

Place a tealight candle on to the black triangle and light it carefully.

> When people came close to Jesus, they changed. They could see things they couldn't see before. They could do things they couldn't do before. They were made well.

> What else did Jesus do?

Place the dark blue and light blue square next to the yellow and black square.

> He told everyone how much God cares for them. He cares for every bird that flies… every sparrow that falls.

Place some small birds on to the light blue triangle.

> And if God cares for the birds of the air, then he cares for people even more.

> Once he showed his friends how much he cared. They were out in a boat on the lake and a great

storm came. They were tossed about on the water and thought they would drown.

Hold a small wooden boat over the dark blue triangle and move it as if on a stormy sea.

But Jesus stood up and ordered the wind and the waves to be quiet.

Place the boat down and hold a hand in blessing above the square.

The more people got to know Jesus—the more they came close to him—the more they knew deep peace on the inside.

Finally, Jesus knew that the only way to repair what had been broken was to go to Jerusalem for one last time…

Place the other green square next to the dark blue and light blue square.

… and let himself be stretched out wide…

Pause, then stretch both your arms out, to the left and right.

…and die on a cross.

Drop your head, pause, and then place a small wooden cross on the square.

It was the only way to bring God close to people and people close to each other.

Trace your finger along the vertical and then the horizontal beams of the cross as you say this.

But three days later...

Place the final yellow square next to the green square.

... people saw Jesus alive again.

Place a wooden resurrection figure of Jesus on the square.

Now anybody who wants to come close to God can do so. Anybody can be part of God's new beginning—part of his new gift—and be full of light, because Jesus, the light for the world, has made it possible.

During these last words, slowly place some small wooden people figures around the Jesus figure.

God did all this because his beautiful world got spoilt. God did all this to clear up the mess that people had made of his gift.

And what God did...

Lift up the manger and baby.

... began with the baby Jesus at Christmas.

The storyteller then shows the children the special little book that they can take home and links some of its pictures to the journey. This will remind them of the things they have seen. They might like to show it to their parents or carers and tell them about the journey.

He then explains to the children that they can take the story with them in a special way. A candle snuffer is held over the burning tealight candle in order to gather smoke. This is then gently wafted towards the children and the storyteller invites the children to carry the story with them as they leave.

The leader then asks the group to leave the living room singing 'Where are you going, children?' as they go (see page 97).

After this, the first group will go on to do the craft activity while they wait for the second group to complete their journey. The second group will then join the first group to collect coats and depart, making sure that the teacher has been given a bag containing their craft work and books. Brown takeaway-type bags are easily purchased from cash-and-carry stores and can be labelled with the school name.

If the budget allows, it is also good to give each school a pack containing the gift of a resource book, such as assembly outlines or Christmas activities, some publicity for forthcoming Christmas events at church and follow-up material if possible. Contact details for ministers, lay workers or children's work leaders who would be prepared to help with assemblies or RE would be valuable if available.

Suggested plan of rooms

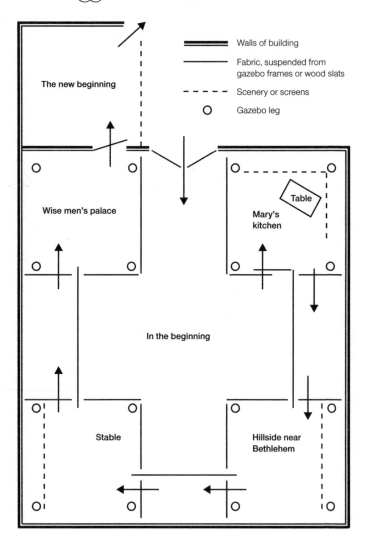

Walls of building

Fabric, suspended from gazebo frames or wood slats

Scenery or screens

O Gazebo leg

The new beginning

Wise men's palace

Mary's kitchen

Table

In the beginning

Stable

Hillside near Bethlehem

Where are you going, shepherds?

Words & Music: Andrew M Rudd

Reproduced with permission from *The Christmas Journey* published by BRF 2009 (9781841016214)

Part Three

*

After The Christmas Journey

Once schools have visited *The Christmas Journey*, there are many ways of using the experience to reach out into the community. If the school is in agreement, invitations can be given to children to come back to an all-age worship service at church, or to bring family or carers along to a public opening of the presentation. Follow-up for teachers can be helpful and the offer of taking a school assembly is often gratefully received. Some ideas for these activities are described below, with more information to be found on the website, www. christmasjourney.org.uk.

All-age service

If appropriate, use *The Christmas Journey* to invite families or carers to an all-age worship service in church on the following Sunday. This is an ideal opportunity to encourage children to bring parents or carers along to church to experience a friendly and enjoyable time that links to the event. It may be possible to leave elements of the scenery and settings in place so that the children are reminded about the story they heard earlier in the week. The service could be planned to include familiar items such as the theme song, but could focus on different aspects of the story of Christmas.

There are many resources available to help with planning a service and much will depend on the style of your all-age worship, traditions and so on. For example, the 'Barnabas in churches' website, www. barnabasinchurches.org.uk, has many ideas that can be adapted to your own circumstances.

All-age talks

Advent: The light that lasts for ever

The theme of the light shining in the darkness is at the heart of the Advent story. The traditional carol service reading from Isaiah 9:2 reminds us that 'those who walked in the dark have seen a bright light'. In Isaiah 60:19 we are told that it is the Lord who will be our eternal light—hence the title of this idea, 'The light that lasts for ever'. Using some simple illustrations, this activity leads into the Christmas truth that Jesus is the light from which all light comes, and builds upon that truth with some prayers for the world, the church and each other to use with your group.

You will need to collect the following items for this presentation: a box of long-life matches; a tealight candle; a long-life bulb; some Christmas tree lights; an Advent candle; a picture of the sun; and some circles of orange-coloured paper (about 10cm in diameter and enough for each child to have one).

Invite everyone to wonder about how long different lights might last. Will any of the following lights last for ever? Strike a long-life match and watch it burn slowly. Then light a tealight candle. Show a long-life bulb and read from the packet how many hours it is meant to last. Introduce some Christmas tree lights: there may be some laughter here because a few bulbs always seem to be faulty, plunging the whole tree into darkness. Or what about an Advent candle, which by now may already have burned down considerably? Finally, show a picture of our own sun—the biggest burning light that we can see clearly. Even this will not last for ever.

Explain that none of these lights, special and beautiful as they might be, will last for ever. But someone in the Bible, who looked forward to the coming of Jesus, describes a different sort of light. This person was called Isaiah and he writes about the Lord who will be 'your everlasting light' (Isaiah 60:19–20, NIV). This is the light that lasts for ever. Repeat this phrase and use it at different points in the presentation as a chorus for everyone to join in.

Explain that Christmas is the time when we remember the coming of the light that lasts for ever. The light that lasts for ever is Jesus. Jesus is the light that cannot be put out. John 1:5 says, 'The light keeps shining in the dark, and darkness has never put it out.' Jesus' light will outlast the sun and the stars. Jesus is the light that lasts for ever.

Hand out the orange circles of paper and explain that from this paper we are going to make different sorts of lights that will help us remember the light that lasts for ever. Explain that there will also be some simple prayers for Christmas time interspersed with the story.

Explain that, first of all, the circle helps us to think of the sun burning in the sky. This is the light that lights up our world. The Bible tells us that in the beginning 'God said, "I command light to shine!" And light started shining' (Genesis 1:3). Later, God created two bright lights—the great light to rule the day and the lesser light to rule the night.

Dear God, thank you for lighting up our world. Thank you for the light that shines in the dark. Take our prayers this Christmas and, like the sun's rays, use them to penetrate the dark and troubled places of our world. Where there is war... fear... and despair... may your people be light in these places. May your bright glory be seen. May the Christmas light that lasts for ever be made known and received in people's hearts across the world. We ask this in the name of Jesus, who is the light that lasts for ever.

Now invite everyone to fold their orange circle in half to create a semicircle. They can delicately tear the rounded edge of the semicircle in a wavy pattern to create a shape like a crown of flames burning. Explain that this represents the combined flames of God's people, lit up with the light that lasts for ever. Jesus said, 'You are like light for the whole world... Make your light shine, so that others will see the good that you do' (Matthew 5:14, 16). We are not meant to hide the light that lasts for ever.

Dear God, may we be light in this area and in the places where we live. May your light be seen and heard as we sing carols and share the story of the light that lasts for ever. We ask this in the name of Jesus, who is the light that lasts for ever.

Invite everyone to fold their crown of flames in half again and re-tear the jagged edges as best as they can to create one single flame. Explain that each one of us can be like a candle lit by the light that lasts for ever. Jesus is the light for the world, the light of his people and the light in the heart of everyone who loves God.

Dear God, we pray for every light here that is burning, but especially those that are burning low at the moment. We hold on to your promise that you will not let a dimly burning flame go out (Matthew 12:20). Keep us burning until the day of that great light when you will come again. Help those who are feeling weak, sad or unwell to be aware of your light burning deep within their hearts. We ask this in the name of Jesus, who is the light that lasts for ever.

Finish by reminding everyone that Isaiah said, 'You won't need the light of the sun or the moon. I, the Lord God, will be your eternal light' (60:19) and invite people to keep their orange flames as a reminder that Jesus is the light that lasts for ever.

Gifts: the real meaning of Christmas

Here is an idea for a Christmas presentation that can involve a number of people, children and adults, as they help the congregation to explore what Christmas is really about.

You will need the nine letters of the word 'Christmas' written on separate pieces of card. It would be good if each letter were also decorated in some way, while still remaining clearly visible and legible. Alternatively, you could use different-coloured tinsel, wrapping paper, holly and so on to highlight and bring out each letter in a festive way. Each letter card should also be numbered on the reverse, clearly enough for the holder to see (only numbers 1 to 8, as the second 's' does not need to be numbered). Once you have the letter cards ready, one further step would be to wrap each one in Christmas paper to create nine 'presents'.

If you have wrapped the letter cards, begin the presentation by inviting children to come out and unwrap a present each, revealing the nine letters randomly. Begin to wonder what on earth this present is all about and how the letters are connected, leading eventually to someone recognizing that they spell the word 'Christmas'. The emerging letters may already begin to spell something else first. However, this will only add to the fun and, in fact, leads into the activity coming. Alternatively, simply hand out the letters randomly from the front.

You have now unwrapped the word 'Christmas', but it means so many different things to people. Now, by calling out the appropriate numbers linked to the letters, ask the card holders to come forward and arrange themselves so as to spell the following words. (Remember, when you are calling the numbers out, the children and adults should be standing so that the congregation can read the words left to right.)

Here are some of the words you can spell, linked to a comment, on which you can elaborate as leader:

Cram: there's such a lot to do now that Christmas is so close.
Charm: there are such a lot of cosy family traditions linked to this time of year.
Cash: Christmas seems to cost more and more each time it comes round.
Trash: the same old television programmes turn up again.
Sham: sadly, we often end up putting on a front and pretending to be nice to people we haven't seen for ages—even our relatives!
Smart: it's time to dress up for those Christmas parties.
Crash: and also a time just to sit on the sofa and sleep!

Hits: listening to music and wondering what will be the Christmas number one.

Trim: or rather trimmings—all the extras that go with the special Christmas meal.

But we know that Christmas is really more than all this. Among all these things, what is it that we are really unwrapping this Christmas? There are some more words hidden here, which might help:

Charts: not the Christmas Top Twenty, but the charts studied once upon a time by some wise people far away in the east...

Star: ... who discovered a new star, which they followed carefully. It led them to...

Him: ... the baby Jesus, lying in a manger.

Christians believe that this is the real marvel and miracle of Christmas, but for most people Christmas is spelt like this... Invite the following letters to come out and stand together: C H R S T S.

So what is missing? The three letters left over should then come out, right to the very front, and arrange themselves to spell I AM.

Ah, I wonder if you can see what is needed to help us remember to unwrap Jesus this Christmas.

Christmas cracker story

Use a Christmas cracker as a visual aid. The bang is the surprise of what God did at Christmas. The hat reminds us of the three wise men who came to seek Jesus. The motto reminds us of God's word, the Bible, where we find the stories about Jesus. The gift reminds us of the presents that the wise men brought. The cracker as a whole also reminds us of the gift that God gave to the world at Christmas— his Son.

Characters in the story

A service can be based around the characters in the story. For example, Mary said 'yes' to God in spite of her youth and the problems and difficulties that her decision would bring. God can use those who obey him in amazing ways. The shepherds were very ordinary people doing a job that many would have considered worthless, yet they were visited by the angels and were among the first to worship Jesus. God does not favour the rich and proud. The wise men sought Jesus; we can seek him, too. The wise men worshipped Jesus; we can worship him, too. The wise men gave gifts to Jesus. What kind of gifts can we give to Jesus?

As well as www.barnabasinchurches.org.uk, there are many helpful websites and publications to inspire a good all-age service. Some seasonal visitors will have very little experience of church, so it is best to keep the service short and use bite-sized chunks of activity. Offering refreshments afterwards, or a simple breakfast beforehand of croissants and juice, will help to make people feel more comfortable. Children love quizzes, puppets and good story telling, so include them if possible.

Links with schools

The Christmas Journey is designed to be an end in itself, but could also be used as a springboard for other links with the schools. Most teachers will welcome follow-up work, offers of help with collective worship (assemblies) and advice on resources to deliver the RE and Citizenship curriculum. If the presentation is held at the beginning of December, the school may be happy for a follow-up act of worship to consolidate the experience for the Year Two children and also to show the rest of the school what Year Two have been up to. Alternatively, a follow-up lesson with Year Two could be considered.

There are countless books and resources to help plan a Christmas assembly. The Barnabas website has excellent ideas for the primary age group and there are several other sites that can be accessed. Books such as *Christmas Wrapped-Up* (Scripture Union, 2003) contain useful songs and stories that can be used to enhance the event. Much will depend on the timeframe required by the school and the ages of the children. The law requires schools to hold an act of worship (broadly Christian) every day, in order to help children reflect on and respond to a spiritual topic. Schools are usually happy to bring in visitors to help with it. It should be remembered that this is not an opportunity to proselytise, although it is acceptable to ask children to reflect on issues and join in prayers if they wish.

A suggested format for a whole-school act of worship

Introduction

In the style of a television interview and using a hand-held toy microphone, ask Year Two children what they remember about visiting *The Christmas Journey*. Allow a short time for answers and help the children to explain the experience to their fellow pupils.

Song: 'Where are you going, shepherds?'

Tell the Year Two children that they are going to teach the song to the school. (If possible, have words projected on to a screen.)

Story: 'The three trees'

Once upon a time, three little trees stood on a hillside and dreamed of what they wanted to become when they grew up.

The first little tree looked up at the stars and said, 'I want to be a treasure chest, covered with gold and filled with precious stones. I'll be the most beautiful treasure chest in the world!'

The second little tree looked out at the small stream trickling by on its way to the sea. 'I want to be a mighty ship and carry powerful kings across the sea. I'll be the strongest ship in the world!'

The third little tree looked thoughtful. 'I want to stay on the hillside and grow so tall that when people stop to look at me, they'll raise their eyes to heaven and think of God. I will be the tallest tree in the world!'

Years passed. The rain came, the sun shone, and the little trees grew tall. One day, three woodcutters arrived on the hillside.

The first woodcutter looked at the first tree and said, 'This tree is beautiful. It is perfect for me!' With one swoop of his shining axe, he cut down the first tree. 'Now I shall be made into a beautiful treasure chest!' the first tree said.

The second woodcutter looked at the second tree and said, 'This tree is strong. It is perfect for me!' With a swoop of his shining axe, he cut down the second tree. 'Now I shall be made into a strong ship for mighty kings!' the second tree said.

The third tree felt her heart sink when the last woodcutter looked her way. She stood straight and tall and pointed bravely to heaven. But the woodcutter never even looked up. 'Any kind of tree will do for me,' he muttered. With a swoop of his shining axe, he cut down the third tree.

The first tree rejoiced when the woodcutter brought her to a carpenter's shop. But the carpenter made the tree into a feeding trough for the animals. The once-beautiful tree was not covered with gold, and not filled with treasure. She was coated with sawdust and filled with hay for hungry animals.

The second tree smiled when the woodcutter took her to a shipyard, but no mighty sailing ship was made that day. Instead, the once-strong tree was hammered and sawn into a simple fishing boat. She was too small and weak to sail on the sea, or even a river. Instead she was taken to a little lake.

The third tree was confused when the woodcutter cut her into strong beams and left her in a timber yard. 'What happened?' the once-tall tree wondered. 'All I ever wanted was to stay on the hillside and point to God.'

Many days and nights passed. The three trees nearly forgot their dreams. But, one night, a golden star poured its light over the first tree as a young woman placed her newborn baby in the feeding trough. 'I wish I could make a cradle for him,' her husband whispered. The mother squeezed his hand and smiled as the star shone its light on the smooth and sturdy wood. 'This manger is beautiful,' she said. And suddenly the first tree knew he was holding the greatest treasure in the world.

One evening, a tired traveller and his friends crowded into the old fishing boat. The traveller fell asleep as the second tree quietly sailed out into the lake. Soon a thundering and thrashing storm arose. The little tree shuddered. She knew that she did not have the strength to carry so many passengers safely through the wind and the rain. The tired man awakened. He stood up, stretched out his hand and ordered the wind and the waves to be quiet. The storm stopped as quickly as it had begun. And suddenly the second tree knew he was carrying the king of heaven and earth.

One Friday morning, the third tree was startled when her beams were wrenched from the forgotten woodpile. She flinched as she was carried through an angry, jeering crowd. She shuddered when soldiers nailed a man's hands to her. She felt ugly and harsh and cruel. But, on Sunday morning when the sun rose and the earth trembled with joy beneath her, the third tree knew that God's love had changed everything. And every time people thought of the third tree, they would think of God. That was better than being the tallest tree in the world.

TRADITIONAL

Remind the children that Christians believe that Jesus died on the cross to make it possible for people to be friends with God. Three days after he died, Jesus came back to life, and Christians believe that he is able to be involved in their lives today.

Response and prayer

Light a large candle. Tell the children that it represents Jesus as the light for the world. Surround the large candle with small tealight candles and invite one child from each year group to come and light a tealight candle from the flame. (Provide a long taper so that they can do this safely.) Explain that, just like the flame of the candle, the story can be passed from person to person and Jesus' love can be shared in the same way.

Ask the children to look at the flames and think about how Jesus' love can be shared. Ask them to think of someone who needs that love—perhaps an elderly relative, someone who is lonely or sad, or a friend who has been hurt.

Prayer

Lord Jesus, thank you for coming at Christmas and for living on earth just as we do. You know what it is like to be lonely or afraid. Help us to show your love to those we know who are in need this Christmas. As we enjoy our presents and happy times with our families and friends, help us to remember how much you love us. Amen

If time allows, sing 'Where are you going, shepherds?' again, or a carol that the children know.

Other ideas for assemblies

The Christmas Journey is best done as a whole in a suitable venue that can be easily transformed into the six scenes. However, if it does not prove possible to bring schools in to take part in the whole journey, an alternative could be to take parts of the journey to them as assembly themes. For example, the first scene could work as a lesson or assembly in its own right, although it may be difficult to set up for more than one class. It leaves the children with questions about God's world, so children could be asked to think further about them. To complete the picture, scene six could be taken back to the school after a few days.

The second scene, in which Mary is baking bread, should be fairly straightforward to take in to school. The theme of the assembly could reflect Mary's obedience to God. Allowing all children to taste the bread could be time-consuming in a larger school, but small bags of bread cubes could be given to each class to distribute later. It would then be necessary to give the children a brief synopsis of the rest of the Christmas story and explain that Mary's obedience made the story of Jesus' birth possible.

The stable scene is ideal as a stand-alone assembly. It would be easy enough to take a sheet or large roll of corrugated card to provide a stable wall for the puppeteers to hide behind. An upright piano covered with a blanket can also be used as a stable wall if available.

The wise men's palace is harder to create in a school hall, although a couple of saris draped on a screen and some eastern props would help to give atmosphere. Costumes, a bag of toys and the three gifts are easily transported and the scene can be used to think about this part of the story. Again, this scene would fit into an assembly about all sorts of people who sought Jesus.

The final scene ('The new beginning') could be a follow-up to a lesson on the first scene, or could stand alone as a post-Christmas lesson or small assembly. As the storytelling moves from Christmas to Easter, the material could also be used at Easter to link Jesus' birth to his life, death and resurrection.

Classroom follow-up

Once children have experienced *The Christmas Journey*, teachers may welcome some follow-up activities for the classroom. These could be as varied and creative as possible. It may be helpful to give each school a follow-up resource pack to use. However, it should be remembered that, although the assembly suggestions could involve the whole school, the follow-up is more appropriate for the Year Two pupils who have attended the original presentation. More detailed plans are available on the website, www.christmasjourney.org.uk.

Curriculum links

In the beginning

- **Art and craft**: Numerous possibilities, including collage with photographs, textiles and so on. Paintings of elements of the creation story (space, land, sea, flowers, animals, water and so on).
- **Performing arts**: Work in seven groups to enact the seven days of creation. Use suitable background music such as *Planets Suite* by Holst or *Vltava* by Smetana. In groups, create a musical picture of the seven days of creation using percussion and tuned instruments.
- **Literacy**: Find descriptive words for parts of creation, and, when thinking about the spoiling of creation, find opposites—for example, clean/dirty and so on. Use the words to write a simple descriptive poem about creation and the ways in which people spoil it. Think of feeling words both for human beings and God in the story.
- **RE**: The story of creation is a Judeo-Christian story. Christians believe that God created the world and asked people to care for it. People disobeyed God by not doing as he asked and spoiling the world, as well as their relationship with God. Discuss with the children how the things they saw and heard in *The Christmas Journey* helped to mend our relationship with God. Christians believe that Jesus was the Son of God, who came to earth at Christmas.

NB: This is only one of the accounts that children will experience about the creation of the world. Other religious holy books will have differing stories. Children will also encounter scientific accounts. As they grow and develop, they will have their own questions and beliefs to work through. The important emphasis here is that Christians believe that God created a perfect world and that he wanted people to enjoy it and look after it. People spoiled that relationship, but Jesus came to restore it.

- **PSHE and Citizenship**: Explore moral choices (doing the right thing). How can one person's actions affect others? How can we make the world a better place, collectively and personally? Study *Allegory of Good and Bad Government* (Ambrogio Lorenzetti, 1338–40), using the context of the school environment. This may promote discussion of how behaviour affects outcome, and stimulate work in Literacy and Art.
- **ICT**: Find out from the Internet about the created world—space, seas, mountains, sun, moon, stars and so on.
- **Science**: Take a walk around the school grounds and find as much evidence of God's creation as you can—for example, flowers, leaves, sunshine, new growth and so on. Draw or write them down. Next, see how many signs you can find of that creation being spoiled—for example, disease on leaves, litter, dirty water and so on. Think of ways in which the school could help to improve the environment.

Mary's kitchen

It is probably more difficult to devise separate curriculum ideas from this story, but PSHE ideas could involve talking about obedience and helping others. Mary sang a song of praise to God when she thought about the angel's news (Luke 1:46–55). Children could be encouraged to write their own song of praise about something exciting that has happened to them.

A hillside near Bethlehem

- **Art**: Paint pictures or create collages of starry nights.
- **Music**: Compose night-time music using tuned percussion instruments to recreate the feeling of a dark starry night, building up to the sound that the shepherds may have heard when the angels came.
- **Drama**: In groups, act out the story, making freeze-frame pictures of the event.

- **Literacy:** Think of feeling words to represent how the shepherds may have felt throughout the story. Use these words to create a poem.

The stable

The children may enjoy making different kinds of puppets to retell the story. Suggestions include shadow puppets (cut out shapes and use on an OHP to tell the story), sock puppets, glove puppets, or paper plate puppets (on sticks with animal faces drawn on).

The palace

- Art and craft: There are a number of creative opportunities here. For example, carry out textile work to explore eastern patterns and design by printing on to fabric (using batik, fabric crayons, paint and so on). Design a room in a palace using paint or collage techniques. Design and make a hat for a wise man.
- Geography: Investigate maps of the Middle East and trace the journey that the wise men may have taken.
- History: How might the wise men have travelled to see Jesus? How long did it take? What would daily life have been like for those who were rich and those who were poor in those times?
- RE: *The Christmas Journey* does not mention the wise men's visit to King Herod and the subsequent escape to Egypt by Mary, Joseph and Jesus. The slaying of the children is also omitted. Teachers may want to add the wise men's visit to Herod's palace in Jerusalem and the family's escape to Egypt, but would need to be sensitive to the more violent parts of the story. However, the whole story could lead to discussion about jealousy, refugees and the question of who Jesus was.

The new beginning

- RE: Most of the final scene deals with significant events in the life of Jesus, such as his birth, growing up, baptism, work, storytelling, care for others, death and resurrection. All these are topics that could be explored further. As well as the more obvious RE connections, there are other issues arising from this scene, such as:
  * Who cares for people who are lonely and those who are unwell?
  * Who looks after the world God made?
  * How do we know about Jesus today?
  * Why did the story of Jesus encourage so many people to believe he was the Son of God that the story has been passed down through so many generations?

Some of these questions seem very big for a six- or seven-year-old to think about, but children of this age are beginning to question the world in which they live and it is good to encourage them to reflect on issues for themselves.

Many of these topics could be developed into a scheme of work based wholly on the final scene. Teachers may be interested in further discussion with the organizers if more help is needed.

INSET

Barnabas (www.barnabasinschools.org.uk), along with many other Christian organizations, is able to provide training for school staff on a wide range of topics. There are opportunities for in-service days for teachers, twilight sessions or days with the children. Please check the website for further information.

✻

Resources

www.christmasjourney.org.uk
Downloads of scripts, photographs of sets and suggested plans for rooms and lighting; also updated resources and further ideas for follow-up.

www.easterjourney.org.uk
The Easter Journey website gives information on *The Easter Journey*, a similar presentation to *The Christmas Journey*, but for Year Five children.

www.barnabasinschools.org.uk; www.barnabasinchurches.org.uk
Ideal for books, resources, ideas and training information.

www.frodshamchurchestogether.org.uk
Ideas and information on how the churches in Frodsham work together.

www.sgmlifewords.com
Information about seasonal booklets suitable for giving to children as a memento of *The Christmas Journey*.

www.scriptureunion.org.uk
Christmas Wrapped Up and other useful books.

www.godlyplay.org
Information about the methodology of Godly Play and storytelling resources.

www.standards.dfes.gov.uk
Up-to-date information about the education curriculum.

www.ccpas.co.uk
Child Protection in churches.

www.theworks.co.uk
Inexpensive art and craft materials.

www.homecrafts.co.uk
Window paints and other useful materials.

NB: Local Education Authorities (LEA) suppliers can provide craft materials, including corrugated card. Most LEAs have resource centres and will frequently give churches trade prices.

www.wesleyowen.com
DVD for creation story: *i Worship@ home, Volume One* (Integrity music) (Quick search number 27591)

T. J. Hughes or large DIY stores
Gazebos. NB: It is recommended that you do not buy gazebos online as you will need to check out the quality first.

www.ikea.com; www.diy.com; www.homebase.com
Lighting and other props.

www.oxfam.org.uk; www.tearcraft.org; www.traidcraft.co.uk
Nativity sets from around the world.

www.puppetsbypost.com; www.puppetsforeducation;
www.onewayuk.com
Puppet suppliers. NB: It is recommended that you use realistic full animal puppets rather than cartoon-style character or glove puppets. Should you require further information about *Christmas Journey* puppets, please contact the Frodsham team: www.christmasjourney.org.uk.

★ ★ ★ Coming soon from Barnabas ★ ★ ★

The Easter Journey

**An imaginative church-based presentation
for primary schools**

Moira Curry and Gill Morgan

The Easter Journey provides an exciting opportunity for church-based children's teams to perform a delightful, easy-to-do presentation to their local primary schools. Aimed at Year 5 children, the material gives pupils and teachers alike a memorable learning experience by unfolding the Easter story through creative storytelling, simple drama and thought-provoking artefacts.

The material includes valuable information for preparing the church and school communities for the event, ideas for team-building, helpful hints concerning practical considerations, clear instructions for setting up and presenting the eight story-based scenes, suggestions for follow-up assemblies and ideas for the classroom. The book is designed to accompany the website www. easterjourney.org.uk.

Published November 2009.

ISBN 978 1 84101 622 1   £6.99
Available from your local Christian bookshop or, in case of difficulty, direct from BRF using the order form on page 127.

★ ★ ★ Also from Barnabas ★ ★ ★

Bethlehem Carols Unpacked

Creative ideas for Christmas carol services

Lucy Moore and Martyn Payne
with BibleLands

This book uses eleven well-known carols that appear in the BibleLands Bethlehem Carol Sheet to explore many different aspects of the Christmas message. It includes ideas to create an imaginative carol service, designed to draw in those attending and provide a truly memorable act of worship.

Linked to the work of BibleLands' Overseas Partners, the resource is packed with interesting facts about the carols, extended Bible references and a wealth of all-age, practical, theme-based ideas for creative storytelling, poetry, prayers, drama and worship. The book is structured using a flexible pick-and-mix formula designed to assist people at all levels of experience with the planning of a carol service. A special section for those under the age of five is also included, making the material suitable for toddler groups, preschool playgroups and pram services.

ISBN 978 1 84101 534 7   £8.99
Available from your local Christian bookshop or, in case of difficulty, direct from BRF using the order form on page 127.

Also available as a pdf download: visit www.barnabasinchurches.org.uk

★ ★ ★ Also from Barnabas ★ ★ ★

Christmas Make & Do

Craft ideas inspired by the story of the first Christmas

Gillian Chapman

Bring to life the Christmas story, with Mary and Joseph, the angels and shepherds, the wise men and the baby in the manger.

Make cards and wrapping paper, decorations, an Advent calendar, Christmas party masks and lots more.

Have hours of fun with Gillian Chapman's imaginative craft ideas.

ISBN 978 1 84101 350 3   £5.99
Available from your local Christian bookshop or, in case of difficulty, direct from BRF using the order form on page 127.

★ ★ ★ Also from Barnabas ★ ★ ★

Through the Year with Jesus

A once-a-month children's programme for small churches

Eleanor Zuercher

In her sequel to *Not Sunday, Not School!* Eleanor Zuercher has developed an exciting further year's worth of themed material—this time based on aspects of the life and teaching of Jesus.

The material is explored through a wealth of creative and interactive activities, with a pattern that enables children to feel involved, whatever their age or level of attendance. Each session is designed to last approximately two hours, although this can be shortened or lengthened according to need. The book is packed with fresh suggestions for Bible stories, practical ideas for creating a display for the church, and a host of brand new craft activities, games and ideas for creative prayer. The material also includes an exciting summer activity programme based on the 'I am' sayings of Jesus.

Through-the-year themes include Baptism, Parables, Jesus' friends, Faith, Blessings, Jesus and me, Prayer, Forgiveness, God with us, Miracles and Transfiguration.

ISBN 978 1 84101 578 1   £9.99
Available from your local Christian bookshop or, in case of difficulty, direct from BRF using the order form on page 127.

Also available as a pdf download: visit www.barnabasinchurches.org.uk

★ ★ ★ Also from Barnabas ★ ★ ★

Footsteps to the Feast

12 two-hour children's programmes for Christian festivals and special times of the year

Martyn Payne

Footsteps to the Feast offers the opportunity to explore the 'big story' of God's purpose for his world and his people through twelve fun-filled two-hour special events. Each programme is packed with tried and tested ideas including icebreakers, team games, drama, music and crafts, all designed to explore the overall theme. At the heart of each event there is space for visual storytelling and reflection.

The feasts and festivals of the Christian year remind us that there is more to life than just the passing of days and months. The idea of special half-day events to mark the cycle of faith provides churches with the opportunity to help children to 'footstep' their way into the faith. A special event may well supplement the regular week-by-week diet, while also enabling churches to reach a wider audience from time to time.

The *Footsteps to the Feast* programmes explore the feasts and festivals of Advent, Epiphany, Candlemas, Lent, Holy Week, Pentecost, Trinity, St Barnabas, Harvest, All Saints, St Michael and All Angels and Bible Sunday.

ISBN 978 1 84101 464 7   £8.99
Available from your local Christian bookshop or, in case of difficulty, direct from BRF using the order form on page 127.

★ ★ ★ Also from Barnabas ★ ★ ★

Creative Ideas for Quiet Corners

14 visual prayer ideas for quiet moments with children

Lynn Chambers

This book offers 14 creative suggestions designed to encourage both adults and children to find space for prayer, by creating a physical prayer space in the home or in a place of worship that can be visited and enjoyed. The materials could be used to form an ongoing sacred space throughout the months of the year or offered at particular times—for example, during a school holiday or a season of the year such as Christmas or Easter.

Each prayer idea uses simple, easily found materials and needs minimal space to create a quiet, reflective corner. All the materials for creating such a space have been carefully chosen to nurture an understanding for both adults and children of what it means to come into the presence of God, to listen and to be still. Alongside the visual tableaux, the book offers practical support to enable people of all ages and abilities to move at their own pace and at their own level into a sense of quietness and prayer.

ISBN 978 1 84101 546 0   £6.99
Available from your local Christian bookshop or, in case of difficulty, direct from BRF using the order form on page 127.

Also available as a pdf download: visit www.barnabasinchurches.org.uk

★ ★ ★ Also from Barnabas ★ ★ ★

A-Cross the World

An exploration of 40 representations of the cross from the worldwide Christian Church

Martyn Payne and Betty Pedley

Around the world today, the cross is, arguably, the one universally recognised symbol of the Christian faith, but this unifying sign has been much adapted, decorated and interpreted to convey particular stories that are dear to the community from which they come.

This book tells the stories behind 40 crosses from a wide diversity of cultures and Christian faith traditions and sets out to promote discussion and debate on why this single historical event continues to exercise such an influence worldwide.

Section One contains stories, information, Bible links, wondering questions and suggested activities on the 40 crosses, as well as photocopiable illustrations of each cross. Section Two contains a wealth of extension material ideal for use in the classroom at Key Stages 1 and 2, in collective worship and in church-based activities, including icebreakers, games, prayers and poems, crafts and session outlines for special activity days, assemblies, holiday clubs and all-age worship.

ISBN 978 1 84101 264 3   £15.99
Available from your local Christian bookshop or, in case of difficulty, direct from BRF using the order form on page 127.

★ ★ ★ Also from Barnabas ★ ★ ★

Living in a Fragile World (pdf download)

A spiritual exploration of conservation and citizenship using the methods of Godly Play

Peter Privett

The story of creation provides us with an ideal opportunity to step back and grapple with some of the most important issues concerning the world we live in today.

This book invites children and adults alike to reflect on the fragility of the earth; to become more aware of the complexity of our interdependent lives and to consider how we might relate to each other in a more sustainable and relational way.

Living in a Fragile World uses three-dimensional materials based on the methodology of Godly Play, an imaginative way of telling Bible stories or presenting parables or lessons about Christian tradition, following the Montessori principles of education. Week by week, the sessions move from the wider planetary view, to the land, to the community, to the self. Each week as the story unfolds, the group is invited to recapture the interconnectedness of all things and thereby something of the vision of God.

ISBN 978 1 84101 727 3   £7.99
Living in a Fragile World *is available only as a pdf download from:*
www.barnabasinchurches.org.uk.

ORDERFORM

REF	TITLE	PRICE	QTY	TOTAL
622 1	The Easter Journey	£6.99		
534 7	Bethlehem Carols Unpacked	£8.99		
350 3	Christmas Make & Do	£5.99		
578 1	Through the Year with Jesus	£9.99		
464 7	Footsteps to the Feast	£8.99		
546 0	Creative Ideas for Quiet Spaces	£6.99		
264 3	A-Cross the World	£15.99		

POSTAGE AND PACKING CHARGES						
Order value	UK	Europe	Surface	Air Mail	**Postage and packing**	
£7.00 & under	£1.25	£3.00	£3.50	£5.50	**Donation**	
£7.10–£30.00	£2.25	£5.50	£6.50	£10.00	**TOTAL**	
Over £30.00	FREE	prices on request				

Name _____ Account Number _____

Address _____

_____ Postcode _____

Telephone Number_____

Email _____

Payment by: ❑ Cheque ❑ Mastercard ❑ Visa ❑ Postal Order ❑ Maestro

Card no ❑❑❑❑ ❑❑❑❑ ❑❑❑❑ ❑❑❑❑ ▨▨▨

Valid from ❑❑❑❑ Expires ❑❑❑❑ Issue no. ▨▨▨

Security code* ❑❑❑ *Last 3 digits on the reverse of the card.
ESSENTIAL IN ORDER TO PROCESS YOUR ORDER   Shaded boxes for Maestro use only

Signature _____ Date _____

All orders must be accompanied by the appropriate payment.

Please send your completed order form to:
BRF, 15 The Chambers, Vineyard, Abingdon OX14 3FE
Tel. 01865 319700 / Fax. 01865 319701 Email: enquiries@brf.org.uk

❑ Please send me further information about BRF publications.

Available from your local Christian bookshop.   BRF is a Registered Charity

Resourcing people to work with 3–11s
in churches and schools

- Articles, features, ideas
- Training and events
- Books and resources
- www.barnabasinchurches.org.uk

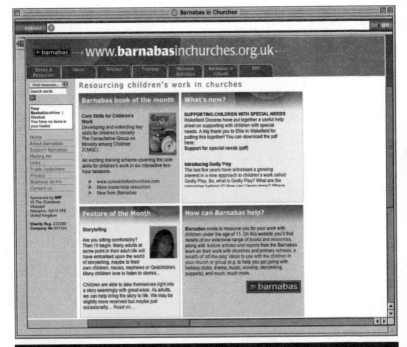